Between Our Hearts

Laura Langa

BETWEEN OUR HEARTS
Copyright © 2022 by Laura Langa

All rights reserved.

ISBN-13: 978-0-578-30114-3

Cover design by: Karri Klawiter

Also by Laura Langa

My Heart Before You

A Guarded Heart

Author's Note:

Although *Between Our Hearts* is about two people in love trying to find their way back to each other, it also centers around miscarriage. Having close friends and family members experience this life-altering loss prompted me to write this book in hopes that this subject might be discussed more openly. Since miscarriage is incredibly intimate and individualized, this novel only represents one couple's fictional experience which I strived to portray with honesty and the utmost respect.

For my parents, Veronica and Karl

·CHAPTER 1·

Sadie strode through the brightly illuminated surgical step-down unit at her usual quick clip, overhearing, "An apple a day keeps me away. Now . . . why would you want to do that?"

Leaning his arm against the wall of a charting enclave, a black-haired doctor stood towering over a young nurse. Her eyes were wide while her mouth was occupied by a substantial bite of a Granny Smith.

Not hitching her pace, Sadie zeroed in on the part of his white coat where his name was embroidered. Above the blue lettered stitches, the insignia for the residents was sewn. He wasn't one of her orthopedic trauma residents. If he had been, he'd be a dead man.

Keep moving. Not your service, not your problem. You've already got a mountain of things today.

"Uhh . . ." The nurse with a blonde bob stalled over her mouthful.

Nope, can't do it.

1

Sadie halted abruptly next to the two. "You know what? No," she said, staring down the resident. Since she was five foot nine barefoot, her black clogs made her easily two inches taller than this troll.

"Excuse me." He raised his eyebrows as he straightened slightly.

"We don't hit on nurses. It's not 1950. She's working. Leave her alone." Sadie's words fell like a surgical hammer on titanium before she checked her watch—ten minutes until she was due in the OR.

The nurse nearly choked, trying to cover her surprised laughter.

His eyes narrowed as he took in her pale green surgical scrubs. "Who do you think you are?"

This was a common mistake made by chauvinistic jerks like him. They saw her without her white coat and assumed she was a surgical nurse. As if female physicians didn't exist.

"*I'm* the director of orthopedic surgery. *She's*"—Sadie pointed to the nurse—"a *professional* on my team who doesn't need to hear your lame come-ons when she's got patients to care for."

The resident's mouth opened, closed, and opened again.

"So if you don't have orders to give regarding a patient, I recommend you find yourself another wall to hold up."

The resident let out a startled exhale, blinking rapidly.

"Anytime now," Sadie urged.

He silently took his hand off the wall and walked away.

"Thanks," the young nurse whispered.

"Don't worry about it," Sadie said, glancing again at her watch before looking into the nearby room. "He's one of mine." She pointed to the patient in the bed. "I expect him to be out of bed and in a chair for breakfast. That needs to happen first thing every morning."

"Oh, okay." The nurse wrapped her apple in a plastic bag and tucked it into her scrub pocket. "Sorry."

Sadie nodded once before continuing down the hall.

◊◊◊

A ten-hour surgical day felt compressed into the time span of a heartbeat, and before she knew it, Sadie was sitting at a table for two in an upscale bar waiting for her friend Parker.

Over the last few years, the long surgical hours had felt like more of a rush than earlier in her career. In the beginning, she'd simply languished in the beauty of surgery, always craving more. More tough cases. More of her hands reconnecting parts of a person's body back together.

Sadie loved working with hardware and all the unfinicky parts of her field, choosing early to specialize as an orthopedic trauma surgeon. Physically resetting pieces of an established skeletal system made a lot more sense to Sadie than noodling around in someone's brain or having to intentionally stop a patient's heart to try and fix it. Give her a shattered person any day of the week, and she'd happily screw and pin for hours.

She often lost herself in the slow, steady beep of her patient's heartbeat as it played a background rhythm to the whir of her bone drill. She never minded the sting of antiseptic that pricked at her nostrils and rarely grimaced when the burnt taste from the cauterizer soured her tongue. It was all a necessary part of the resulting satisfaction of realigning two, or more, bone pieces and restoring them to their formerly whole state.

Sadie's stomach twisted as she tried to ignore the *real* reason she wished she had more time in the artificially lit, reassuringly icy rooms of the OR. There, she was in her element, and each decision came to her like breathing. Automatic. Instinctual. Effortless.

At home, it felt like instead of putting things back together, everything kept breaking apart. Especially now that she'd seen that blue cross telling her she was pregnant again.

She and that blue cross had developed a tormented relationship.

The glimmer of excitement that should have accompanied a positive pregnancy test had been immediately decimated by fear. Because of this, she'd decided not to tell her husband, Clark, right away. Sadie didn't want to watch the hopefulness in his breathtaking blue eyes turn over to despair—the same emotion that seemed perpetually etched into her organs.

In a moment, however, she'd have to share the news with Parker. Sadie had exactly enough time to run her hand over her lavender blouse in an attempt to settle herself before her friend walked to the table.

Truthfully, Parker only walked in the hospital; when she was out at night like this, she *sauntered*. Parker's favorite thing was to discard the dark long-sleeved T-shirt she wore under her surgical scrubs and showcase the extensive artwork on her body. Parker loved the shock factor. When her long, dark brown hair was tied into an efficient knot at the back of her neck, no one knew that most of the skin under her cuffs and beneath her scrub pants was inked with intricate images.

Tonight, her tattoo artist's hard work was evident as Parker wore a barely-there sleeveless mini dress with a squared neckline. Complex images decorated her arms, legs, and even the tops of her toes peeking through strappy heels. She slid onto her high-top seat as their already besotted server followed close behind.

"Hey," he breathed.

"Sazerac, thanks."

The twenty-something hovered, eyes glued to Parker, and cleared his throat. "And for you, ma'am?"

Sadie tried to hide her cringe at the word ma'am. "Soda with extra lime."

He blinked and turned in halting degrees before seeming to regain his focus once Parker wasn't in front of him, burning out his retinas.

Parker waited until he was ten feet away before reaching over the wooden tabletop to grip her hand. Softer brown eyes caught Sadie's and held them silently. She didn't need to speak. Sadie not ordering her standard Vesper was all Parker needed to hear to know that Sadie was going into proverbial battle again.

Over the last eleven months, this had been the third time that Sadie had ordered soda with extra lime. Each time after, within weeks, she was ordering her Vesper with hollowed resignation.

When the bridge of her nose congested and liquid sheened her eyes, Parker released her grip. Sadie knew her friend didn't want to be the cause of her spilling water all over the table.

"Do you want to talk about it?"

Sadie shook her head.

"Do you want to hear about the pretzel boy from my last call night? Riding a motorcycle drunk with no helmet, the idiot." Parker rolled her eyes.

"Yes. Tell me," Sadie said eagerly.

Most people thought her penchant for the gruesome was distasteful, but Parker's smile only lifted because she *understood*. There was nothing more beautiful than taking a nearly dead, broken person and putting them back together.

Five years ago, when Sadie was called for a consult in the ER, Parker was the lead trauma surgeon on the case. Within seconds of excitedly talking over each other regarding the best way to fix the smashed woman's body, a kinship had been formed. They'd also bonded over the fact that they were the only female surgeons in their respective services.

When they'd gone to medical school, statisticians had boasted that fifty percent of graduates were women, but when it broke down into specialties, most of those new female doctors went into pediatrics, obstetrics and gynecology, or dermatology. Not that there was anything wrong with any physician's choice of practice, but it was just more than eighty percent of orthopedic surgeons were men—similar numbers for trauma surgeons. But like Sadie, Parker didn't shy away from a fight, and they'd both tenaciously clawed their ways to respective successes at Durham Medical Center. A little more than a year ago, Sadie had broken two barriers, becoming not only the first female orthopedic surgery director but the youngest, at thirty-eight.

Parker barely lifted her eyes to the salivating server when he dropped off her drink but stopped to say thanks amid the long list of broken bones meticulously detailed for Sadie's benefit.

Already Sadie was fantasizing about the myriad ways she'd have fixed each break as Parker continued with the quick, abbreviated medical jargon-laden speech that would've made an intern's head spin. To the casual eavesdropper, they might as well have been conversing in an alien language.

"Excuse me," a handsome man in his mid-forties wearing an immaculate three-piece suit interrupted.

Parker gazed up with irritation before her look morphed into something slightly softer. "Hello."

"I can see that you ladies are obviously busy, but I wanted to give you this." He slid a slick business card on the table-top in front of Parker. "My cell's on the back."

Parker's eyes darted to it briefly before returning to his. "I'll take it under consideration."

The man's confident smile rose. "I look forward to hearing from you."

Parker unabashedly watched his toned backside as he walked away.

"You're going to climb that, right?" Sadie asked.

"*Sadie Love Carmichael*. Saying such things about other men. You're a married woman," Parker teased.

Sadie rolled her shoulders uncomfortably. "Yuck. You had to middle-name me?"

Parker's grin only widened. Early in the relationship, Sadie had revealed over too much gin that she hated her name.

Well . . . she'd always liked her last name and had come to grips with her first, but *Love*? What kind of person gave their child a name like that?

Her mother, that's who.

The woman who, after three strapping boys, had been pleased as punch that she'd finally gotten her southern doll to dress up. Except Sadie had never fit the mold her mother had tried to shove her into. She'd always preferred scrounging in the mud with her brothers, bringing home toads in pencil boxes, and wearing pants to the frilly, poofy things her mother insisted she wear.

Also, she'd never been small, never been ladylike. She was curvy instead of thin, assertive instead of demure, and her shock of auburn hair always announced her entrance to a room. Her mother didn't hide the fact that she felt Sadie was a grave disappointment.

In her stronger moments, Sadie would tout that she didn't care. But no matter how strong you are, your parents' opinions matter. Fortunately, her father had been her champion from the first time she'd doggedly held her ground as a pint-sized toddler, always calling her "my girl" with affection. Enduring her mother's criticism had been so much harder in the six years since her father had died of a massive myocardial infarction.

"How are you and Clark?" Parker asked, rotating her lifted glass in a circle.

As Sadie tried to sort out an answer to that weighted question, her mind snagged on the fact that *Love* was also Clark's pet name for her. But his use of it was the only time it felt right. The first time it'd dropped from his lips—before he'd even *known* her middle name—vibration had zinged down her spine and settled heavily in her quads. A month later, when he'd discovered her full legal name, he'd only chucked that breathless laugh of his and whispered "perfect" into the crook of her neck.

Absentmindedly, the back of her index finger traced the space that lit with awareness from her memory.

"That good, huh?" Parker's voice and eyes were gentle.

Her hand dropped as a crumbling sigh left her body. "This whole thing"—she roughly waved over her flat belly under her slacks—"is hard on us."

It's hard on me.

Since their friendship was built on a mutual understanding of female strength in the face of adversity and a love of fixing broken people, talking about their feelings wasn't part of the zeitgeist. Addressing emotion in general wasn't one of Sadie's strong suits, and therefore she tended to avoid it all together.

Parker nodded silently while taking a sip from her drink. Sadie hadn't touched hers yet, and condensation started to pool around the base. To give her hands something to do, she plucked the limes from their space bobbing in the clear bubbles and squeezed each wedge in half.

"I'd offer advice but it's out of my realm, and I wouldn't want to assume." Parker fingered the intricate fern leaves wrapping her collarbones.

"And I appreciate that." Her gaze lifted to her friend's. "I just don't feel like talking about it tonight."

Or ever.

Parker's chin dipped sharply once. "I had a twenty-year-old with sixteen GSWs last week."

Sadie felt her shoulders relax before she brought her drink to her lips.

·CHAPTER 2·

Clark plucked another succession of strings with his fingertips, nearly failing to move his hand over the neck of the hand-me-down guitar at the appropriate times. Propped against a low bookshelf, a tablet continued with the chords of the song he was supposed to be playing. But his hands froze as he listened to the low rumble of the garage sounding from the other side of the house.

Almost immediately, his heart ran in two opposing directions. It clenched with the desire to see his beautiful wife, to spend time with her, to be close to her, but at the same time, it ached with trepidation of what would instead be his reality—terse conversation and her avoidance.

Clark let out a deep nasally breath as he leaned the guitar against the wall. Picking up the warm wooden instrument from a secondhand booth at the Northwood Farmer's Market a few months ago had been an impulsive purchase. In their small eclectic town outside Durham, the market had been a mainstay even before he'd begun taking their two-and-a-half year old daughter, Lottie, when Sundays stopped being family days.

This evening, he'd stumbled over the chords that his learn-to-play-guitar app had displayed for him to follow. At least when he was faltering over trying to coordinate his fingers to work in a way to produce sound in an appealing manner, his mind wasn't dwelling on the fact that his life was falling apart. Lately, it had almost been a game to keep at bay the deep ache that twisted at the base of his chest.

Wake up and ignore the fact that even though Sadie's calendar said her first surgery was at nine, she'd already left the house by seven.

Halfway through the increasingly rare family day at home, saying "Sure, love" when she claimed she needed to go to her office on the hospital campus to finish charting and emails, though she'd always done it from home before.

Lay down for sleep and fight the raging desire to simply hold her between his arms and whisper "I love you" into the crook of her neck, and instead toss a resigned "Goodnight" over the distance she'd created by facing away, clinging to the edge of the bed.

Often, he spent his solitary evenings reading webpages about how to support your wife through recurrent miscarriage instead of his usual stack of non-fiction books. But it was a rare moment when anything he said or did seemed to make a difference. He was walking through a minefield and never knew what action or word would set off an emotional explosion, further damaging their threadbare relationship.

And the unfair thing about it was that all he wanted to do was to walk *with* Sadie—to hold her hand and face this together, but after the first loss, she'd closed herself off, and these days, it was impossible to reach her.

The sound of cabinets opening and closing and the pouring of cereal into a bowl reached Clark's ears before he turned the corner to their kitchen. His lip reflexively quirked at the corner. When they'd first met, he'd been surprised to learn that she often subsisted on cereal. Whenever they'd spend time together, he'd be sure to feed her, but even after coming home from a delicious meal, she'd sometimes pour herself a bowl of cereal for dessert. It had been a topic he'd tease her about, and the opportunity to do so now sent effervescence searing through his veins.

"Are we going Fruit Loops or Apple Jacks?" He held his smile and breath as he took a step into the room decorated in warm tones.

His wife's pale green eyes darted up mid-pour, and then she did the most incredible thing: her lips broke into a relaxed, wide grin. "Cocoa Puffs and Kix mixed."

Clark's breath left his body as he tried to steady himself against the stumbling of his rapidly beating heart. It didn't matter if she was in scrubs, a T-shirt and shorts, or the ethereal lavender blouse she was wearing now. Sadie stunned him. Every time.

Every. Single. Time.

He loved her mid-length auburn hair all knotted and wild first thing in the morning. Or when she'd forgotten to take off her scrub cap and a deep line impressed the smooth skin of her forehead. Or when she was covered in dirt in the backyard, Lottie in her lap, the two of them making mud pies on plastic plates after a summer rainstorm.

He loved her so much that most of the time it hurt.

Keeping the casual lift of his lips, Clark crossed the hardwood to her. To be safe, he stopped kitty-corner, and firmly planted his hands on the center island. He wanted to gather her to his chest and kiss her until that subtle flush pinked her skin. He wanted to hear her squeal as he tossed her over his shoulder and carried her to their bedroom.

Internally, he shook himself.

Right now, she was happy. She usually was when she came home from time with Parker. His only goal was to keep her in this mood for as long as he could.

"I'd better make sure that's not poison." He swiped her spoon and had the bite of freshly milked cereal in his mouth before she could protest.

"*Hey*." A playfully annoyed look scrunched her brow, and he worried his chest would explode. "That's my snack."

"Oh, you want it back?" He asked over his huge mouthful.

Her face pinched as she squinted her eyes shut. "You're gross."

"I can't believe the woman who rearranges broken bones all day can't handle someone talking with their mouth full."

One hand covered her eyes as the fingers of her other groped around in the air to snatch back her spoon. "Give me back my spoon."

Her fingers finally found the silver object, but they also gripped his in her blind attempt at retrieval. His pulse hammered in his throat at her accidental touch, and he didn't miss that her lips parted from beneath her held hand as a near silent sigh left them.

Quickly, he rearranged his fingers so his pinky gripped and held her wrist in place.

Her hand fell from her eyes. "Clark, I'm hungry."

"So am I." The second the husky words left his lips, he internally scolded himself. She'd make that *I'm pissed at you* face and sulk away now.

Instead, she took a rapid succession of shallow breaths, her eyes growing slightly wider.

Tread lightly. Taking their joined hands, he placed a featherlight kiss over the inside of her wrist.

When her thick eyelashes fluttered closed at the touch, gratification roared through him. He heard the clattering of the metal spoon on the granite island before he realized he'd dropped it in favor of framing her face with his hands. Her lips came willing to his as a soft moan vibrated against his mouth.

Expletives tore through his mind as he backed her against the refrigerator, pressing his full weight against her. The contact of her soft, warm skin against his made every single cell in his body scream *finally*. He angled her face, exploring her mouth with deep strokes of his tongue, and rejoiced when her tongue raced to do the same.

Over the last few months, she'd stopped kissing him. If he did initiate a kiss when she got home, she'd only reluctantly peck him back. On the rare day that his wife was home all day, they'd often wake up and go to sleep without their lips touching once. It was in stark opposition to the passionate kisses they'd shared early in their relationship or even for the first year and a half of Lottie's life.

When Sadie's hands framed his sides and ran up his ribs until her short fingernails dug into the muscles over his back, the low resonant growl that escaped his throat was reflexive. He let his fingers fall to her hips to reposition her, to align their bodies in that way that always seemed like the closest he'd ever get to perfection. As he did, a taped-up scribbling of Lottie's fluttered to the ground.

He could feel her hesitation, as if the movement of the paper hitting the floor was bringing her back to reality, but he fought against it like a man walking upstream in a raging river. Relinquishing his grip on one hip, he brought his palm behind her bottom and pulled her even harder into him. Her moan bouncing around in his mouth made him lace his other hand through her hair.

"God, Sadie." His tongue wove around hers again. "I've missed this."

The switch was instant. Her body sagged against the fridge as her fingers fell from his shoulders.

Shit. No. No. No.

They'd had sex two weeks ago, but it hadn't been like this. It'd been perfunctory, as she'd been ovulating. After sex, she'd balled into a position to help her conceive, instead of letting him hold her against him, and then taken a shower.

It wasn't an unreasonable thing for him to say that he missed her. It had been two weeks, after all. But they both knew that the breathy way he'd whispered it into her open mouth meant he missed her wanting this as much as he did. That he missed the way they used to be before trying for Lottie's sibling had become more challenging than either of them had anticipated.

He felt his hands loosen as she pulled away. "I've got an early case in the morning. I should get some sleep."

His chest felt as if it was tearing into sixteen distinct pieces as he stepped back.

Her face pinched as she moved to pour the full bowl of cereal down the drain. Metal blades cutting through softened cornmeal reverberated in the silent room. She turned off the disposal but didn't move from her position in front of the sink.

Crossing the room more cautiously than he would if he'd encountered a frightened and injured animal, he came to stand behind her. When her head bowed, he couldn't help running his palm down the defeated curve of her spine as his lips met the back of her skull. She didn't move or flinch, and he allowed himself to wrap his arms around her, gently pulling her back to his chest.

Sadie melted into him, closing her eyes and resting her cheek against his. He wanted to tell her that he loved her more than anything but worried that even saying that would break the tentative moment of peace they found themselves in. Instead, he watched her beautiful face in the reflection of the darkened window over the sink. Mostly her forehead was slack and relaxed, but occasionally it would tweak.

He didn't know what was running through her mind, but he knew she wouldn't tell him the truth anyway. Her refusal to talk to him, to let him share those burdens with her, tore at him more than each loss they experienced. Her not trusting him was excruciating.

Taking a deep breath, he kissed the crook of her neck before stepping back. Holding her was all that he'd wanted a moment ago, but now it'd become so painful that he just couldn't be near her anymore. Her surprised eyes blinked open as he resisted the urge to rub his hand over his throbbing chest.

"I'll let you get some sleep."

Her lips downturned. "What are you going to do?"

"I started a project in the woodshop during Lottie's nap that I'd like to finish tonight."

When they'd bought this house a few weeks before their wedding, it had needed a lot of work, but Clark had happily taken on the project. It had given him something to use his skills as a custom carpenter once he'd decided to stop working full-time and stay home with Lottie. The first thing he'd done was take the extra detached garage and turn it into his dream woodshop.

Slowly over the last three years, he'd customized everything in the home and restructured the layout of several rooms. He'd even redone the entire deck and built Lottie a personalized playhouse in the yard. Now that their home was perfect, he felt at a loss. He'd always figured he'd go back to work part time when Lottie was in school, but right now that was several years away.

Taking Lottie on their Sunday morning stroll through the farmer's market had actually sparked an idea in him. The weekly market occupying the largest parking lot at the end of the town's quaint main-street style small-business area had lots of farm stands but also tents for the mom-and-pop coffee shop, the secondhand store, an indie bookstore, and several different artisans. Clark usually enjoyed chatting up the blacksmith, who was a staple next to the apiary owners.

During their last conversation, he'd admired an intricate wall hanging commenting on how it would fit perfectly between the shelves he'd just finished in the den. The more the conversation evolved, the more he ended up sharing about himself and his listlessness now that he didn't have a project to complete. When Thatcher had offhandedly mentioned that he could do woodworking, Clark had laughed it off. That day he'd bought the guitar.

But the conversation had run through his mind so many times over the lonely weeks following that he'd ended up looking at different projects online. Geometric wood art wall hangings were quite popular right now, and with his skillset, they'd be incredibly easy to produce.

"Oh, okay." Sadie's eyes flicked to the ground.

"*Sadie.*" Her name was an exhausted exhale. "Do you want me to come to bed with you?"

All she had to do was say yes, to ask for what she wanted, to *Talk To Him*, and he'd do it. But it hurt too much to guess and then get it wrong and be rejected over and over again.

"No." He felt her word like a two-by-four to the side of his skull. "You should finish your project."

He waited a beat before he said, "All right."

She nodded to the ground.

His step back punched him in the stomach, but he forced himself to turn and walk out of the room.

·CHAPTER 3·

Hooking her keys on the custom organizer Clark had built in the mudroom, Sadie kicked off her ballet flats. Out of habit, she ran her hand tenderly over her husband's construction. Some of the yellow pollen from the opening of the pinecones remained on her fingertips. The dust was impossible to avoid mid-April in the south, and it had stubbornly infiltrated the mudroom by wafting through the garage door.

She slid her shoes into the shoe rack built below the cushioned bench, taking the time to line them up nicely though for years she'd just tossed them in a heap by the door. When she straightened, Lottie's yellow rain slicker and matching boots caught her attention. Guilt tightened her ribs.

It had been a challenge not to head to one of her places after leaving the office today. Most residents of their town would see them simply as well-planned green spaces, but for Sadie the Northwood parks she frequented were outdoor sanctuaries she could run to when her emotions threatened to overtake her.

Though the pull had been magnetic as she drove, Sadie had managed to grip the steering wheel and keep herself from using the turn signal in the wrong direction.

Today she needed to go home and spend time with Lottie. She needed to try and push everything else aside and be present with her daughter.

In the past, time with Lottie had always included Clark, but with the way things were between them, she just couldn't take the broken way her husband looked at her.

So the idea of "Mommy/Daughter time" had surfaced in her mind. Growing up, her mother, Penelope, had forced Sadie into shopping and beauty appointments. As an adult, Sadie's nails were often shorter than most mens', and she'd always been too pragmatic to fuss with or keep up polish. And with the ease of online shopping, Sadie hadn't stepped in a clothing store in years.

Sadie often worried that the activities she engaged in with Lottie—mostly of the playing outside variety—were in some way exerting that same unrelenting pressure Penelope had pressed on her shoulders over the years.

Intentionally straightening her spine, she mumbled, "My relationship with Lottie isn't the same as the one with Mama. I let her be who she is."

As she dropped her work bag next to her desk, a ripple of anguish whipped through her looking at the place where she'd first miscarried. The pain had seared through her insides more powerfully than any cramp while she had been finishing charts one lazy Sunday evening. She'd called out for Clark in a voice so panicked that at the time, she hadn't recognized it as her own.

He'd been at her side in a breath, holding her, supporting her, asking with a worried look in his eyes if they should call for a sitter and go to the ER.

Even in that moment, she'd known in her bones it was over—this hollow awareness resonated deep in her marrow. Medical training had nagged in the background as well, knowing the words her OB would tell her would mirror the ones she'd told anxious families in the OR waiting room when a patient didn't pull through.

Sadie's hand flew to her belly, reminding herself that it wasn't an automatic this time. This time, things could be different.

Please stay with me, she begged the tiny life inside her.

Each loss hit Sadie harder than the last, making her pull back from everything in her life. The cruelness seemed exponentially difficult to bear after the effortless way Lottie had been conceived.

Sadie stared in disbelief at the blue cross staring back at her.

There's no way this is happening, *she thought.*

There's no way that after nearly two decades on the same birth control, it had failed her at the ripe age of thirty-five, seven months into the longest relationship she'd ever had. She'd never even planned on having kids. She and Parker had an air-tight plan to be the kickass spinster aunts in each of their families.

The fact that she didn't want a family and Clark—who was currently whistling while washing the breakfast dishes just beyond the closed bathroom door—did was one of those deal breaker situations. But neither of them had addressed it yet. Everything about their relationship had been so hot and so fast that she figured when the intensity died down in a few months, they'd eventually get to the reasons that they shouldn't be together long-term.

Except now she had something very long-term building cell-upon-cell inside her. Something that would eventually outlive her. Her open palm stifled a small, squeaky sound trying to escape her mouth.

Shaking her head, she told herself to get a grip before wrapping the pregnancy test in an excessive amount of toilet paper and shoving it to the bottom of Clark's trash. She splashed another round of cold water over her face before opening the door to Clark's kitschy one-bedroom apartment.

His toned and tanned bare back shifted as he did a little dance while scrubbing the skillet he'd scrambled eggs in. Paint-splattered sweatpants hung loosely over his hips.

"I'm pregnant." The words burst from her, prompting her to cover her subsequent gasp with her palm again.

The plan had been to wait until she could confirm with an ultrasound or something more scientific like a blood test. It'd been a while since medical school, and she didn't really remember much of her OB rotation, but she was pretty sure store bought pregnancy tests weren't one-hundred-percent accurate.

Clark's brilliant blue eyes flipped over his shoulder before his whole body turned. Soapy bubbles from the sponge dripped down the skillet and onto the floor. "You're kidding?"

Sadie could only shake her head.

A laugh burst from him as he took a step toward her before noticing his occupied hands. He returned the items to the sink, turned off the water, and hastily dried his hands on his pants before sweeping her skyward.

Her brows pinched together from her space near the ceiling. "You're not upset?"

Clark's arms loosened slightly and gravity took over, allowing her to slowly slide against his firm chest until her toes touched the ground.

His bright, excited eyes met hers. "No, this is perfect."

Before she could answer to the contrary, his mouth was over hers. It was several minutes later before he allowed her to catch her breath, darting away to his desk tucked in the corner by the window. His hand obscured the view of the object he retrieved from the top draw until she could feel his breath on her face again. Within the small velvet ring box sat the most beautiful cushion-cut diamond on a rose gold band.

When her eyes flitted up to his, he smiled, the dimple in his left cheek deepening.

"See, I told you it was perfect."

Sadie took a halting breath, shaking off the memory and continuing upstairs. After getting changed into jeans, a light sweater, and sneakers, she found Clark and Lottie in the backyard. A grey and black soccer ball was between Clark's broad hands behind his head, his elbows bent in preparation to throw it. His Adam's apple was prominent as his chin jutted up, apparently looking for something in the branches of the many sweetgum maples lining the edge of their grass.

At last, he tossed the ball, and it hit a thick branch thirty feet above him. Several hundred tiny, light pink objects began pinwheeling down to the ground. Lottie squealed as she ran to get beneath the natural confetti, dancing as they showered down on her. Sadie arrived at her daughter's side in time to catch three of the fluttering objects in her upturned palm. Seed pods. She ran her thumb over their slightly iridescent winged shape, and they fractured in her hand.

"Mama!" Lottie hugged her shins.

Sadie picked up her daughter, nuzzling into her soft curls. "Hi." The more and more she closed herself off, the more she missed her daughter's smell, her daughter's voice, her daughter's touch. "I missed you," she whispered.

"We didn't think you'd be home this early." Clark's edgy voice pulled her attention.

His eyes were cautious as he spoke, dark eyebrows holding a slight pinch.

It'd been more than a week since they'd kissed in the kitchen. Ever since, she'd been working nearly non-stop to avoid being alone with him. To be fair, he'd been spending more time in the woodshop, even though he claimed that he'd finished the repairs on the house months ago.

"I thought I'd leave early."

Clark's face visibly relaxed, and the smile that had often lived on his face before everything went complicated returned in full force. It felt as if Lottie had accidentally kicked her in the stomach.

It was staggering sometimes how attractive her husband was. He kept his dark, nearly black straight hair neat on the back and sides, but longer and careless over the top. When the breeze played with it like it did now, it made her finger's itch to race over his scalp. Though he'd always been fit, he'd packed on even more muscle since becoming a stay-at-home dad and attending Dad Bod Fitness classes six days a week. After she'd picked "the hottest guy in the room" to kiss on a lark the day they'd met, it still baffled her that he was still with her.

When it felt overwhelming, Sadie found herself focusing on the little imperfections that made him real. Like the slight, almost imperceptible crookedness of his nose, or how his collarbones were somewhat uneven, or the thin white scar that ran the line of the left side of his jaw from a years-ago accident at work. Right now, that jaw was covered with several days' worth of dark stubble. Her brows twinged—he'd always shaved every morning.

"After we're done chasing seed pods, I thought we'd have a fire. It's probably the last cool day to have one." Clark gestured toward the built-in stone firepit and surrounding seating area. Wood had been stacked into a triangle in preparation.

"Oh." She glanced at Lottie, who was happily sucking the first two fingers of her left hand. "I thought I'd spend some time with Lottie. Maybe take her to the park? Like a mommy/daughter date?"

Clark winced at the word date. The features of his face hardened as his gaze fixed over her shoulder. "You should. You guys never get time alone. I could use a break anyway."

Her stomach dipped. "You're sure?"

"Just take her to the bathroom first." He bent to pick up the soccer ball. "We're potty training now. She's in big girl undies."

An invisible hand clenched and twisted her intestines. Being unaware of this change in her daughter's life made the guilt she felt earlier magnify tenfold.

"See." Lottie pulled at the waistband of her leggings to reveal rainbowed training undies.

"You've been doing a great job today, little love." The blatant affection in his voice made Sadie's skin feel scrubbed raw. "No accidents."

"I big girl," Lottie beamed.

"Yes, you are." She tightened her grip on her daughter, kissing her cheek. Sadie's lips came back tasting of blackberry jam. "Okay." She bounced Lottie a bit on her hip, stalling.

"See you when you get back." Clark turned his back to her, disassembling the wood and stacking it neatly in the nearby woodpile.

Sadie would've liked to think she did a decent job of pushing the interaction with her husband from her mind while she played with Lottie on the Peaceably Park playground. She followed her daughter through the small playground meant for two-to-five-year-olds, going down the four-feet-long barely inclined slides, over and over. It was when Lottie was happily being pushed in the bucket swings that her mind flashed back to the cutting glint in Clark's eyes.

Since she'd been volunteering for extra call shifts and helping Vinay, the new residency chair, in addition to taking more time to herself, she'd been leaving Clark home almost exclusively with Lottie. Their daughter was pretty easy-going as far as toddlers went, but she still required a lot of attention. Maybe he was feeling burnt out from essentially being a single parent. A plan formulated in her mind, and by the time they got home, just in time for Lottie to use the potty again and keep her dry streak, she'd decided to broach the subject after bedtime.

Though Clark had already made dinner, Sadie insisted on doing all of Lottie's nighttime routine herself. Clark came into their daughter's room for stories, and they sat, three in a row against Lottie's toddler bed, reading before putting her to bed.

Once the door had been shut on their daughter's room, she spoke. "I want to talk to you about something. Do you have a minute?"

Clark eyed her while leading them to their bedroom. "Sure."

"I've been thinking about all the things you do for Lottie, for me, and I want you to know I really appreciate all the sacrifices you've made for us—"

"Taking care of our daughter is not a sacrifice. I'm her father." He folded his arms over his blue half-zip sweater.

A strangled exhale left her lips. "That's not what I meant. What I'm saying is because of my hours, you're with her a lot. You seem to be really tense lately, and I thought maybe you could use more of a break. We could put her in a preschool program or maybe get a nanny."

Clark pinched the bridge of his nose, and that simple action told Sadie she'd said the wrong thing. "I don't need a break, Sadie. I need you to talk to me."

He'd nearly yelled the last three words, so she moved to close their bedroom door. "I am talking to you."

An irritated half-laugh burst from his lips. "No, you're not."

"What do you want me to say? Do you want me to say that I feel like I'm being shredded internally because I *literally* am? Life is being ripped from my body, forcing me to deal with the bloody aftermath, and there's nothing I can do about it." Her voice broke.

"*Love.*" His anger vanished as he took two large strides toward her.

"Don't." She stepped back. Everything felt itchy and barbed, and she didn't want to be touched.

His arms fell to his sides as pain rippled through his eyes.

"It's *horrible*. It's horrible and it's hollowing and . . ." Sadie felt as if her chest was cracking open. If she didn't stop now, if she didn't tamp down the emotions threatening to devour her, she wouldn't survive. "It's something I don't want to talk about."

He sighed. "Then I don't know how we're going to be able to fix this." His arm swept between them.

A tightness pinched in her stomach. "I just can't."

The emptiness she felt seemed reflected on her husband's face as he ran a hand through his hair.

Several long, extended, excruciating seconds passed in absolute stagnant silence. Her shoulder twitched as she longed for the jarring alarm bells of a surgical case gone wrong—anything besides the silence of their hearts drifting farther apart.

"I need to—" he began.

"Finish a project in the woodshop," the whispered words were aimed at her feet.

"*Sadie*." Her name sounded like pain.

She'd schooled her features before she raised her face. "I should get to bed anyway. I have a lot of things to catch up on tomorrow because I took off early today."

Clark stared at her for two heartbeats before his shoulders dropped. "All right, love."

She tried not to flinch at his use of her pet name. It didn't seem like an appropriate title now.

He cautiously left their room, his footfalls sounding heavy as they descended the stairs. She tried to keep things together while she went through the business of washing her face and getting ready for bed. Only once she was tucked between the covers, her back facing Clark's side of the bed, did she let the sorrow she'd barely kept at bay swallow her whole.

·CHAPTER 4·

Lottie babbled from her position in her orange jogging stroller as Clark held the three mid-sized projects under his left arm. He navigated through the crowded market straight to the black-topped canopy tent emblazoned with *Thatcher Daniels' Smithery* in orange flamed lettering. Thatcher met him with a broad smile over his thick, slightly grey-streaked beard and once Clark had engaged the brakes on the stroller, a hearty handshake.

"I see you took my advice to heart." Thatcher nodded to the collection under Clark's arm.

Clark rotated the stack of inlaid woodwork pieces so the blacksmith could see the top one. He'd started small just to see if this was something anyone would even want, making three rectangular wall art pieces sized at eighteen inches by three feet. The top one had two chevrons coming from the right and left side near the top and the bottom of the frame with horizontal pieces filling the gaps to the point of each chevron. In between the points, he'd laid the slivers of wood at a diagonal. He'd alternated between clear pine and stained knotty hickory to create more visual interest.

This piece had been ridiculously easy, and he'd finished it in mere minutes—a design he could mass produce quickly. It was the third piece under his arm that made an unanticipated unease sweep back and forth between his shoulder blades.

"What do you think?"

Thatcher motioned for him to come around to the back of his tent. "I think I want to see the rest."

He set the first one down against the leg of Thatcher's U-shaped display to reveal the next—an intricate mosaic design. This one had taken him slightly more time to create.

"These are great." Thatcher ran his hand over the smooth, finished surface. "You should talk to Robin about having your own tent."

"You think so?" Clark asked.

"Definitely. I think you could easily sell these. And this market is one of the better ones. I've been at a bunch of different ones over the years that were hostile and not enjoyable to be a part of. Everyone was always jockeying for the best location or trying to steal business from other vendors. I'm too old to put up with crap like that." He chuckled, rubbing his hand over his messy salt and pepper hair. "I just want to make things and sell them, not deal with drama."

Clark guessed that Thatcher wasn't a day over fifty and easily had the chest and arms that any twenty-something would envy. Even being a thirty-five-year-old who exercised almost daily, Clark couldn't help feeling a twinge himself.

"All right."

"How much did these cost to make?"

"Uh." His brow pinched before he laughed. "I honestly don't know. Most of the wood was leftover from other projects. Why?"

Thatcher grinned. "You should know the cost to help you decide pricing."

"Oh, right." The materials and labor to produce these was negligible. Right now, producing these pieces gave him a much needed distraction. Any income he received from them would be a bonus.

"Not knowing about your raw material cost, I'd guess you could price these at a hundred a piece." Thatcher lifted the second piece to reveal the third. "Easily one-fifty for this one. Maybe two-hundred."

The wood frame in Thatcher's rough hands looked almost like a cross section of a nautilus shell, only instead of curved lines, it had been created with perfect matching angles. Dark stained wood was laid to be the lines of what would have been the shell, and bright seamless pine was meticulously layered into the spaces in between.

"Isn't this a fractal?"

"Yeah. The math on that one took a little longer."

Thatcher blew out a low whistle. "Nice."

His stomach dipped seeing someone appreciate his craftsmanship on something that he considered out of his realm. He was used to perfect lines and exact construction, working within a finite space and budget, and meeting his client's requests. He'd exceeded expectations often enough that he'd been requested by name on seventy percent of the projects he'd done with a local high-end design company before becoming a stay-at-home dad. These new projects, however, ignited a different part of him, leaving him with this strange, exposed sensation.

He straightened. "How do I get in contact with Robin?"

Thatcher gestured to the far end of the market. "She's the owner of the organic soaps tent up front."

Clark had smelled the various scents wafting from the pastel-toned tent he'd passed by many times but had never stopped to look.

"All right, great. Thanks."

He tucked the pieces under his arm and steered Lottie toward the entrance to the market, but when he got to the tent, no one was there. His head spun, searching for the owner, as Lottie started to fuss in the stroller.

"All done." Her little chubby hands pulled at the five-point restraint over her chest. "*Down.* Down, now!"

Normally when they went to the market, he let Lottie meander through the tents and then carried her when she got tired. When he'd pulled out the stroller from the back of his slate-grey RAM Tradesman truck this morning, Lottie had whined and fought him until he'd bribed her with a fruit snack. The empty wrapper sat between her sneakered feet as she threw her full twenty-five pounds against the harness with a grunt.

"Oh, sweetheart. Do you need a bunny?" A smoky voice came from behind him.

A woman who smelled of lemon crouched in front of Lottie, handing her a small rag doll bunny with a purple felt flower stitched over the center of its belly. His daughter gasped with joy and clenched the toy to her chest.

"Wabbit." Lottie giggled and made the beige bunny dance on her knees.

When the woman, drowning in frumpy neutral fabrics, rose to standing, Clark was shocked to find she was only in her late twenties. Thick, curly strawberry-blonde hair seemed to have a mind of its own as it traipsed down her back to the base of her spine. Six different colored stones were strung around her neck, each dangling from its own chain. Like Sadie often did, this woman wore no makeup, and her light blue eyes were excited as she placed a hand to the side of her mouth, leaning in conspiratorially.

"It's an aromatherapy bunny. The belly is filled with dried organic lavender to encourage calmness. I recommend warming it in the dryer before bed for a no-fuss bedtime and sweet dreams."

"Thanks," Clark said, getting his bearings. He'd half expected the organizer of the farmer's market to be someone Thatcher's age or older. "How much is it?"

She waved a hand with at least seven rings on it. "This one's on me. Just tell your friends if it works for her. Word of mouth is worth more than money."

Everything cleared as that strange déjà vu feeling filtered away to understanding. From her energy to her dress, Robin reminded him of his mother. A strong punch rocketed through his belly. His parents had been asking for a few weeks if they could come down for a visit, but each time, he found an excuse to decline. He didn't think Sadie would be up for company, even though she got along well with both his mother and father. Not for the first time, the heaviness of dealing with his grief in isolation pressed down his spine.

The truth of it was his parents could have provided the support he'd been missing during this period of uncertainty and sorrow had they known what he and Sadie were going through. They were no strangers to heartache but always worked as a team through it. Something he and Sadie were not anymore.

When his mother had been diagnosed with breast cancer the summer of his sophomore year of college, Clark and his father had immediately rallied around her. Clark hadn't even thought twice about dropping out of his architecture program and taking a carpentry job to help Dad pay his mother's medical bills. He'd moved home and done whatever was needed when he wasn't working: cooking, cleaning, laundry. After a year of chemo, radiation, and surgery, her scans had finally come back clear. By the time they could all take a breath, Clark had found that he really liked working with his hands instead of drawing beneath the artificial lights of the design studio, and he'd never gone back.

Robin's gaze caught on the wood pieces beneath his arm. "Those are fabulous. Where did you get them?"

He tugged at the back of his neck with his free hand. "I made them."

"Really?" she said as he handed them over. "Are you interested in selling them?"

"That's actually why I'm here." This strange, nervous laugh came out of his mouth.

"You're an incredible artist," she mused, focusing on his second piece.

As much as he agreed the finished products were aesthetically pleasing, he wasn't sure if creating three panels of multi-angled wood qualified him as an "artist."

"Thatcher recommended I speak to you about getting my own tent. I'm a carpenter by trade, but I have time on my hands right now for other projects," he said as she set the second piece against the stroller.

Her fingers delicately ran over the nautilus piece, contemplatively tracing the innermost part of the design. "Thatcher's absolutely right. You should sell with us. Our little community could use a woodsmith."

Setting the last piece down, she brightened as she continued. "The contract to join is online. NorthwoodFarmersMarket.com. Just print it, sign it, and bring it back to me. It's three-hundred dollars for a space for the season, and we run every Sunday morning rain or shine until October 31st. You'll also have to obtain and display your North Carolina sales tax license." She put her index finger on her chin as her eyes drifted off. "I think that's it. If you have any questions, you can email me." She handed him a business card with a splashed pastel paint design—bars of soap in the corner, her name and contact information in the center.

"All right." As his tentative idea became a living, breathing thing before his eyes, the trepidation he'd felt earlier wafted away in lavender-scented waves.

Her eyes were drawn to the nautilus piece again. "I simply adore this one. The different tones of the wood make it look almost three dimensional."

"Keep it. Maybe just send some people my way when I get my tent up." He felt his lips rising in a smile. "I hear word of mouth is worth more than money."

Robin wrapped her shawl-covered arms around herself with a wide grin. "I had a feeling I was going to like you."

·CHAPTER 5·

"Screwdriver."

The comforting weight of the requested tool landed in Sadie's outstretched palm. She flipped it, adjusting her grip before driving the last screw into the plate she'd placed, reconnecting the separated sides of her patient's ulna. The basic ORIF surgery was one she did often because people often broke either one or both of their lower arm bones when bracing a fall.

Reagan, the chief resident at her elbow, wordlessly removed the reduction clamp. A twinge of shame whirred up Sadie's fingertips because she should have let Reagan set and screw the steel surgical plate, but her antsy hands hadn't relinquished a tool all surgery. To her credit, Reagan didn't complain. She simply assisted, performing the role Sadie should have taken since Reagan was only months from graduation.

Repairing this man's severed bone was the only thing making Sadie feel in control at the moment. Setting plates and screwing segments back together was something she could do without disappointing anyone. She ran her gloved fingertips over her handiwork, completing the final inspection of the surgical site, when an agonizing rip tore through her lower abdomen. The cramping squeezed and twisted, forcing her to bow toward the pain. Liquid quickly sheened over her eyes, and the surgical field blurred.

It was happening again.

And there was nothing she could do.

Nothing anyone could do.

She was utterly helpless.

Before, the pain had come and gone like contractions, but this time it was constant, radiating from her belly and wrapping around to her back and down her thighs. A sharp breath drew into her lungs as her internal muscles squeezed again, forcing her hands to still.

"Dr. Carmichael? Is everything okay?" Reagan asked.

Sadie blinked twice, careful not to spill the tears pricking at the edges of her vision, and slowly straightened her spine. "Do you think you could finish this case?" she asked, knowing Reagan was more than capable.

"Yes, ma'am."

"Then I'm going to step out. Page me if you have any issues."

Sadie was able to keep a calm mask on her face until she opened her OR locker, and Clark and Lottie's smiling faces beamed back at her. The home-printed picture was centered on a sheet of printer paper with *We love you, Mommy* written in Clark's hand above Lottie's pudgy, slightly smeared handprint in orange washable paint. Sadie bit back a sob as she grabbed her messenger bag, shoving back the crumpled patient notes threatening to spill onto the floor.

Once alone in the single use bathroom between each entrance to the locker rooms, Sadie confirmed what she already knew.

She'd lost her.

Sadie knew it was weird that with each cross of blue lines, she immediately assigned a gender to the small ball of life within her, but it was automatic. She'd done the same thing with Lottie and been right when they'd found out on ultrasound that she was a girl.

She rummaged through her bag to find a thick pad, knowing that each time she went to the bathroom, she'd have to see the evidence of the heartbreak she'd just experienced in the OR. In a more merciful world, losing a child wouldn't have such a visual reminder for days afterward.

When she stood up, pain wracked through her body, streaking white behind her shut eyelids. She leaned heavily onto the sink basin and ran the water full blast to cover the choking sound of her tears.

The medically trained part of her mind logically told her that the child she'd just lost wasn't even a child, wasn't even a *she*, but an embryo—a collection of cells less than six weeks along, the very beginnings of life. But Sadie knew in her heart that was wrong. *She* was her baby. A potential sibling for Lottie. A person to complete their little family.

Sadie pulled a bundle of paper towels from the dispenser and used them to swab her face. The messenger bag tipped over, sending several thick pads sliding across the square-tiled floor.

Her emotions swung briskly as she kicked at the plastic-wrapped bundles of cotton. Then she was pitching the almost featherlight objects with hurricane-force intensity against the staff notification bulletin board on the wall. After three or four throws, she slid to the ground, chastising herself for having the adult equivalent of a two-year-old's tantrum.

Breath heaved in and out of her body, but she felt detached, almost like she wasn't there in the room. Her mind focused instead on the disappointed look that would cross Clark's face, how the lower lids of his eyes would sag, and his mouth would turn into that deep frown that mostly covered it nowadays. She pulled her knees into her body, hugging them tight before remembering that she didn't have to say a thing because this time she'd kept the positive pregnancy test from him. Maybe tonight when she got home, it wouldn't be an emotional hellscape.

Maybe.

Each time she miscarried, she failed at giving Clark the one thing he's always said he wanted. Early on in their relationship, he'd been earnest about his desire to have a family with at least two children. He'd been the lonely only child of busy, intellectual parents, and the area where he had grown up outside Baltimore hadn't provided him with neighbors his age.

What if, now that she'd failed again, there was nothing left of her that he wanted?

Sadie knew she was smart, hard-working, and one of the best orthopedic surgeons at Durham Medical Center, but she'd always worried that on some fundamental level she'd upset the scales of the universe by marrying Clark. That nagging voice telling her that she should have listened to her mother's chiding words, warning her that she wasn't wife material—*mother material*—crept down her spine.

For the first few blissful years of her and Clark's relationship, she'd blocked that thought out because they'd been happy. She loved Clark more than she ever thought possible, and he seemed just as crazy about her. Things were so good that Sadie could put away all the persistent thoughts that she wasn't the kind of woman men married.

Clark didn't seem to mind that she was too direct and self-assured. He never balked at her hours or dedication to her career. And he had been the one to suggest—and then seemed to enjoy—being a stay-at-home dad. They'd been in their own little bubble of happiness. There were days when she'd carelessly think, why can't this be the way to have our family?

When they'd gotten pregnant their first month of trying when Lottie was nineteen-months-old, she'd felt like she was thumbing it to her mother. Even after throwing up in the morning, she'd brush her teeth, and Clark would rub her back and then press her against the counter, almost making her late for work.

Unlike her pregnancy with Lottie, when she'd been nervous about becoming a mother, this time she'd been excited. She'd actually looked forward to feeling those first flutterings and kicks, to the adoring way Clark would gaze at her when she had a full belly. But eight weeks later, she'd lost that baby, and everything changed.

Sadie was uncertain of how she'd made it through evening traffic, only recognizing that she'd entered the quiet streets of her Durham suburb—or town, as the locals liked to call it. When her mother's caller ID showed up on her Toyota Rav4's console, bile flicked at the back of her throat. Pulling over, she waited for the call to ring to voicemail before texting a message stating she was still at the hospital and would have to call her tomorrow. Penelope didn't like it when she didn't answer their scheduled call, but Sadie wasn't going to talk to her mother within an hour of her third miscarriage.

When her head lifted from her phone screen, she finally noticed her surroundings. The carved wooden sign for Peaceably Park stood just beyond her passenger window. Sadie's forehead clunked against the steering wheel as a heavy pressure threatened to crumble her bones.

Two months after her first miscarriage, she'd found herself at this park, tucked into a ball, sitting in silence, trying to process the tumultuous emotions that still pulled at her. Her gaze had fallen upon a tenacious dandelion flower stretched toward the setting sun. The jovial yellow of its petals had soothed something that had been scratching at her. It was the first time a smile had organically crossed her face. The first time she'd felt lightened.

She'd argued with Clark on the way out of the house the next day and found refuge in that same park after work, but this time the flower had been mowed down. There was no thinking. Only movement. Action. Response. It had been a numb experience, like someone else had temporarily taken control of her body. She found herself at the local mom-and-pop hardware store, trying to ignore the woodsy scent that reminded her of her husband, buying a single pot of gerbera daisy—yellow for the girl she'd lost.

Back at the park, she'd wandered around for an immeasurable amount of time before the scrubs covering her shins became stained with dirt. She tore at the ground with her bare hands, and it wasn't until she pressed her fingers against the top of the plant, rooted safely in the ground, that a miniscule fragment of peace laced through her.

That was when her first tears fell. Almost as if to water the little life she'd just secured in the sandy loam. She'd allowed herself to succumb to the emotion that had been ripping her insides apart for weeks. Only she hadn't known she wasn't alone.

"Honey, you can't—" The hoarse rasp of a woman's heavily accented words preceded her mentholated cigarette scent. "Oh." Seeing Sadie's tear-streaked face, unease quickly rippled over the woman's features. She tugged at the elbow exposed from her green Northwood Park Services button-up tucked into dusty khaki work pants.

Sadie frantically wiped at her face to destroy the evidence of her untempered display of emotion. Only her hands were caked with soil, so the dirt simply mixed with the liquid salt on her cheeks.

"That's not—" The woman in her early sixties blew out a breath and doubled back to the small gas-powered utility cart parked nearby. "Here." She thrust a mostly clean hand towel at her.

The scent of sweat and cigarette smoke overwhelmed Sadie as she swept it over her face. A nauseating cough left her throat before quickly holding the towel back out to the woman. The older lady did a hesitant lunging step to grab it, as if Sadie was something feral.

The setting sun sliced at Sadie's eyes as her gaze remained trained on the woman's well-worn work boots. "Do I have to take it out?" She tried to keep her tone even, but her voice cracked.

The silence that hovered was so extended that eventually, she was forced to raise her face. The woman's overly bleached hair and heavily tanned skin sagged from days of hard work in the sun. Her left fingers tapped out an incoherent rhythm on the seam of her pants over the birdsong through the trees.

The woman's face pinched. "What's under it?"

"Nothing."

Her eyes narrowed. "If you buried a cat or dog in there, it'll just get dug up by some critter at night."

A short, forceful exhale made a painful sound as it rushed over Sadie's teeth.

Burial.

Her eyes squeezed shut as understanding dawned. That was why she was here. Why she was caked in dirt and tears. Why she was on her knees when she otherwise commanded every aspect of her life.

Death didn't care if you've worked your whole career to thwart it. It'll hit you just as hard as the next person. Her shoulders tightened at the irrational thought that maybe she'd brought this upon herself—upset some cosmic balance by doing what made her the happiest.

"What's it for, then?" The woman's gruff question helped pull her from her tailspin.

Sadie only shook her head. She'd been unable to talk to Clark about what had happened, even though he kept trying to bridge the subject, so she couldn't open her soul to a stranger. Her gaze dragged from the woman's weathered face to her own hands—capable hands that now shook like those of an unhinged person.

"It's all right." The woman's calloused fingers were on her shoulder with a sturdy grip. "We'll leave it. Ain't no good being the head groundskeeper if I can't make decisions like keeping a little ole flower." Her next sentences were like the soft rumble of thunder in the distance. "It can stay. I'll tell my crew not to touch it."

"Thank you," squeezed out of Sadie's tight throat.

The woman stepped back, looking away. "Name's Deborah."

"Sadie."

Deborah nodded and took a few paces toward her utility cart before turning around. "If you cover the soil up with the mulch, it'll keep the moisture in. And don't be surprised if the flower's wilted for a few days. Transplanting shocks 'em a bit, but she'll bounce back."

Another tear escaped with the word "she'll," but Sadie managed a comprehending nod before she pushed the mulch back into place, the sound of the cart driving off registering in the periphery.

Tomorrow Sadie would have to buy another plant and place it next to its siblings. Her abdomen cramped again, dragging a mournful cry from her mouth. Within the safety of her parked car, she could vocalize the pain ricocheting through her body—through her heart. Once the cramping subsided, she pushed away the wetness from her face. It was only two more miles home. A place that had once been a refuge but now felt like a warzone. With a heavy sigh, Sadie shifted into gear.

·CHAPTER 6·

"Then hippo went 'Ahhhh!'" Clark flipped the grey stuffed hippopotamus upside down midair and thumped his head on Lottie's bed as his daughter burst into giggles. "Hey!" he said in his squeakiest voice. "Why did you throw that banana peel at my feet?" The stuffed monkey in his right hand tilted his head in a semblance of a shrug.

"Bad ooo-ahh." Lottie smiled.

"You're right, little love. He's a very bad monkey." He set Hippo in his lap to wave a scolding finger at her stuffed monkey.

Lottie's little lips tugged higher before she sighed and flopped back on her pillow. Clark felt his face mirroring her expression as he ran his fingers through her mop of auburn curls, mostly dry after her bath.

Most of the guys he used to work with had balked at his decision to not put Lottie in day care and return to a jobsite. They couldn't imagine that his chest filled to the brim daily at spending his hours playing with and taking care of his little girl—that he actually enjoyed supporting his wife in her dedication to her career. That he found Sadie's strength incredibly sexy.

Over the years, Sadie had often complained about the toxic patriarchy she'd slammed up against time and again to fight for where she was. She had one male colleague, Josh, who was affronted at her being the director of orthopedic surgery. Since Sadie had been the lone woman surgeon in her specialty for years, she was ecstatic that Reagan, the chief resident and Sadie's mentee, had just accepted the orthopedic department's offer of employment.

Unfortunately, Clark had seen that same gender imbalance in his line of work as well. Though he'd always treated the female contractors he'd encountered with the same respect as their male counterparts, he knew most of his co-workers often didn't. If that disrespect happened in front of him, however, he was the first to say something about it. He wouldn't have been his mother's son had he not.

His parents had often touted there was no problem blending in with the culture you were submerged in, but that didn't mean you needed to propagate its negative stereotypes. So Clark did what he'd always done when working—he'd been a chameleon. He'd shown his tougher exterior and filled the expected role of "carpenter" when at work and allowed himself to be who he really was at home.

Not all the guys were bad, though, and Clark continued to meet up over beers every few weeks with the ones he'd been closest to. The after-work Friday night ritual used to be a weekly routine for him. They'd shoot the shit about their lives for a few hours, half-looking at each other, half-watching whatever game was on the thirty-plus screens at the sports bar they frequented. More often than not, Clark would have to suppress a smile at his friends' gratuitous displays of masculinity.

The garage door opened and closed over the whisper of the white noise machine on the bookshelf, hitching a slight pause in Lottie's lullaby. Clark's shoulders tightened before he took a conscious breath to loosen them and continue singing.

If Sadie wanted to, she'd come in and give their daughter a kiss, but sometimes his wife felt it was better not to rile Lottie up right before bed. And sometimes after a long surgical day, Sadie didn't have the mental energy to deal with anything when she came home. The door never opened, so Clark snuggled with Lottie until her little body heaved with sleep before slipping from her bedroom.

Steam billowed once he opened the door to their large master bathroom. Inside the shower, water bounced at errant angles off of Sadie's bowed head, the hot liquid darkening her auburn waves and pinking the pale skin of her body.

Her defeated posture meant one of two things—she'd lost a patient in surgery or she'd miscarried today.

She'd been trying to hide the fact that she was pregnant for the last two weeks. She'd obviously taken the pregnancy test at work because the two that he'd bought at the store were still under the sink. But since they'd been tracking her cycle to try and maximize conception over her window of ovulation, he'd noticed when, during the week when she should have had her period, tampons hadn't littered the bathroom trash can.

Clark slipped out of his sandals and opened the glass shower door. His wife's forehead wrinkled with exhaustion at his unexpected presence behind her.

"It's been a—"

"I'm fully dressed, Sadie." Only then did she notice that the scalding water was wetting his T-shirt and gym shorts. "I'm not trying anything. It's just your shoulders are so high they're brushing your ears. Here"—he gripped her skin and began massaging with firm, even strokes of his fingers—"let me help."

Sadie's head fell into the spray again as her tight muscles sagged under his attention. Her whole body seemed to relax at his touch and damned if satisfaction didn't sprint through his veins. Everything between them had been so tense for months, and in this quiet moment, tranquility swept the moisture-filled bathroom. Eventually, she inched her way back until she was almost leaning onto him, the water pelting her stomach.

"See." He couldn't help but kiss the wet strands of hair over her neck. "That's better, isn't it?"

Her languid nod brought a smile to his lips before his gaze swept downward. Though his intentions had been pure when he'd entered the shower, the flushed quality of her naked skin drew his attention, and he let his eyes linger on her shapely bottom.

Early in their relationship, she'd slept in these slippery nightshirts that always seemed to creep up in the middle of the night. She'd also had a tendency to wrap a leg over the top of the covers. Waking up to the lacy edges of her underwear peeking from the duvet had been his absolute favorite thing. He'd even started setting his alarm a half hour earlier to allow time to take advantage of that gorgeous sight.

Clark was contemplating letting his fingers dip down for a handful when his wife's words made him freeze.

"I lost her," she whispered.

He opened mouth to ask for clarification when she turned in his arms.

Her pale green eyes bore through him. "I'm sorry."

Clenching pain ripped through his chest as understanding smashed at his brain. *Again. It happened again.* He wanted to drop to the floor of the shower and drag his knees to his chest, but Sadie's haunted eyes were still watching his. Like the other times, he packed up his emotions and put them in a box.

He brought her to him, gripping her tightly. "It's not your fault, love."

Clark expected her to stiffen, to push him away like she'd done the first two times. To tell him she needed space and then not talk to him for days except for the necessary parental exchanges. To never *really* talk to him about how she was feeling, even though ever since the first miscarriage, grief had gripped him so strongly that he felt he was chained to a boulder as he walked through his day. Lottie's smiles and giggles would extend the chain by a few feet, but then he'd stumble upon the box of toys they'd stored away for the next baby, and it'd shorten to a few inches.

But Sadie didn't.

His strong, boss-surgeon wife crumpled onto his chest and wept so savagely in his arms that he felt as if his entire world was being decimated. The pain he'd experienced seconds before was insignificant compared to the unthinkable torture of his own powerlessness in the face of Sadie's heartbreak. His hand found the back of her head as he clung even tighter, kissing her forehead.

Each time this happened, helplessness raged through him like a violent and angry dragon. Its scaly claws ripped at his organs; its sharp teeth devoured him from the inside out. Though he was useless in the face of Sadie's anguish, at least this time she was letting him hold her.

When the heaving of her slippery shoulders evened out and her breathing slowed, his mind raced to find something soothing to say, but all it fixated on was how they couldn't go on like this.

"Maybe we should take a break."

Her swollen eyes flashed with irritation as they pulled away from him. "I'm thirty-eight. Things are only going to get harder the longer we put it off." Being of "advanced maternal age" weighed heavily on Sadie's mind.

Hesitantly, he opened his mouth.

"Don't." Her eyes shot daggers at him as she took a huge step back. The water sprayed between them, and she batted at the showerhead to push the flow against the wall.

His lips pressed together and creased into a frown. He'd made the mistake of bringing up adoption a month ago, and she'd had a reaction just like this. He didn't see any issue with giving a good, loving home to a child who needed one, but Sadie only saw that option as failure. And if there was one thing Sadie didn't do, it was fail. She'd conquered every difficult obstacle in her life, and in her mind, she was going to overcome this.

Except maybe this wasn't something she could strong-will her way through.

Crossing her arms over her chest, her eyes slid to her feet. "I need to finish showering."

The bones that protected his heart felt like they were splintering.

"Sure." His hand found the handle to the door before he stopped, swallowing against the thick saliva clogging his throat. "I love you."

Sadie's dewy lashes blinked, but she didn't raise her gaze. "I love you too."

Clark didn't stop to strip his clothes or dry off. He simply grabbed his towel, wrapped it around himself, and raced to the back deck. Later, he'd go back and mop up the water from his footprints, but right now he needed to drag clear air into his tight lungs.

The fickle southern spring was in a mood today. It'd been nearly eighty degrees and sunny yesterday, but today it hadn't peaked over sixty. He'd put Lottie's aqua puffer in the coat closet earlier this week only to drag it back out on their way to Dad Bod Fitness class this morning.

He felt the cool deck boards beneath him before he realized he'd collapsed on the top step, cradling his head in his hands. When Sadie's body had heaved irregularly against his moments ago, he'd had to stop himself from finding solace in her breakdown. It felt perverse, but since it was the first time he'd seen her cry, a part of him had almost sighed with relief.

At last, they were going to discuss the boulder that had pushed itself between them. At long last, she'd shown him she was as emotionally eviscerated by this as he was. He'd foolishly thought that they could finally work through their sorrow together instead of drifting further apart.

But then she'd pushed him away.

Again.

A halting breath left his lips as he raised his face to the dark backyard. The crisp breeze blew over his saturated clothes helping clear his mind.

He couldn't do this anymore.

He couldn't function in a vacuum, even though he knew Sadie didn't want their families to know that they were having issues.

He'd overheard Jayce talking about going through a miscarriage with another dad the other day at class. Even though it was a betrayal of the trust of the woman he loved more than anything, he needed to be able to talk to someone. He needed to not feel so alone in this.

Standing up, he stripped off his wet clothes under the bright moonshine—one of the bonuses of living on five acres that was mostly forest. Once he'd toweled himself completely, he went straight to the garage. The plastic bin that held the accessories for Lottie's swim lessons also included his trunks. After pulling them and his boots on, he hung up his wet clothes, pushed out the side door, and padded across the cement driveway to his woodshop.

Though his bare chest and fingers felt numb, he turned on his miter saw and started cutting slivers of reclaimed wood into exact angles. Knowing that in a few hours, when this piece would be complete, he'd find Sadie already asleep in their bed.

·CHAPTER 7·

Sadie knelt in the damp grass surrounding the dark hardwood mulch, dewdrops and dirt marring her black slacks. The last two times she'd done this, she had found some solace in the action, but this time, only a crushing sensation pushed at her spine.

After replacing the mulch around the yellow gerbera daisy, she gathered her trowel and the plastic pot. Deborah would drive by sometime later this morning when the park officially opened and find this third flower. Sadie stood, unable to tear her gaze away from the yellow-white-yellow trio planted in the ground. Only the beeping of a horn as someone locked their car in the parking lot jolted her from her rumination.

A heavy sigh left Sadie's lips. She needed to leave now to make her first appointment on time. Maybe staring at the grey X-ray images of her patient's bones would help distract her from the insidious blackness overtaking her heart.

Thirty minutes later, Sadie's nurse aide, Klara, handed her a tablet displaying her first patient's X-rays. "Thirty-five-year-old female fractured third through fifth lesser metatarsals. Dr. Harvill wanted to be sure that she didn't need a pin in LM4. DOI was two days ago. Patient states she tripped in the yard chasing her toddler."

Her eyes flicked over the images on the screen, easily identifying each break. Three clean, simple fractures stared back at her. Her patient didn't need surgical intervention, but apparently Dr. Harvill was feeling nervous about his diagnosis. Sadie's brow twinged with irritation. "I'm assuming she's been booted since then."

"Yes, doctor."

She knocked twice before pushing the exam room door open, leaving Klara on the other side. "Good morning, Johanna. My name is Dr. Carmichael—" She glanced up from flipping through the electronic chart, and the rest of her typical introduction died in her open mouth.

Klara had forgotten to mention that her patient was roughly thirty-nine weeks pregnant. Even though Sadie knew that particular bit of her patient's history was irrelevant to her foot fracture, the sight of the taut fabric of her patient's maroon maternity shirt stretched over her rotund belly snapped the breath from Sadie's lungs.

She forced her eyes back to the tablet as the splintering pain started in her chest and then thickly swept through each of her bones. Her entire body struggled to keep her suddenly heavy frame standing. Even her fingers ached.

Turning her back to her patient, she flicked on the faucet at the small stainless-steel sink. While washing her hands, she forced herself to swallow over the lump in her throat and continue. "I see you broke your foot. Can you tell me how it happened?"

Her patient let out a large sigh. "I was in the front yard with my two-year-old, Graham, and the trash truck came by. He got so excited and raced toward it, and I was afraid he'd run into the road, so I sprinted as best I could to get to him. He stopped on the sidewalk, thankfully, but not before my foot got caught in a divot between the grass and the concrete."

Sadie nodded to the upper cabinets above the sink as she took her time drying her hands with crisp paper towels. "And how have you been managing your pain since then?"

"Just Tylenol and ibuprofen."

She straightened her strong shoulders and faced her patient with an empathetic expression. Unfortunately, any other patient would have been given some variety of narcotics, but Johanna's pregnancy precluded her from that. "I'd like to remove the boot so I can examine your foot. Normally, I'd ask you to get on the exam table, but if you're comfortable in that chair, we can do it there."

Johanna's lips twisted in a regretful grin. "You'll have to do most of it. I can't really reach my feet right now."

"I understand. That's not a problem." Sadie perched on the hard dark blue chair next to Johanna and reached for the Velcro fasteners of the orthopedic device, focusing solely on her patient's foot. "You've been wearing this the whole time since the break? Even at night?"

The ripping of tiny plastic teeth sounded over the whooshing of the air conditioner.

"Yes."

"Good."

When she leaned to get the fasteners over the top of her patient's foot, she brushed up against Johanna's belly. A hot spike of unwelcome envy stabbed her in the ribs as a halting breath left her nose. She should have moved the chair to sit across from her patient, not beside her.

"I'm sorry if it smells," Johanna said timidly.

"It's not—" She stopped as a tiny foot pressed through the woman's strained skin into Sadie's side.

"Xavier!" Johanna playfully scolded her belly. "Don't kick the doctor."

Her patient chuckled lightly until Sadie sat straight up, completely abandoning her task while brushing the hot tears that had escaped from her eyes off her nose.

"I'm sorry," Sadie squeaked.

A flush ran over Sadie's cheeks and down the part of her neck that was exposed through the one open button of her black dress shirt. She'd thought she'd gotten through most of the tears this morning in the shower, but here she was losing it in front of a stranger.

The impulse to run was fierce, but Johanna's hand was on her back in an instant, rubbing smooth reassuring circles. "It's okay."

The dynamic shift was so stark that her right temple pulsed with pain. *She* was supposed to be helping this woman, not the other way around. Here she was supposed to be a professional, not the fragile woman who was barely making it through her days. Sadie made another sloppy attempt to clear the liquid that kept streaming from the corner of her eyes, blatantly disregarding her internal commands for it to cease. Johanna added soft shushing sounds to the gentle pressure of her hand.

"I don't normally fall apart in front of patients. I'm usually completely in control . . ." Her gaze unwittingly dropped to Johanna's belly, and that pressure in her chest built again.

"You've lost a baby."

A messy, choked sob was her only response. Her quads tensed as she pushed against her feet, but Johanna's outstretched arms caught her before she could flee. That itchy impulse faded in her patient's tight embrace, and she found herself giving in to the sorrow that haunted her, ungraciously wetting the back of Johanna's soft cotton T-shirt.

"I'm sorry." Sadie scrubbed at her eyes again, exhaling loudly.

"There is no need to apologize. I *understand*." Johanna gripped her tightly before leaning back. The look in her patient's eyes was the same one she saw in the mirror each morning.

"How—" The breathy word escaped before she stopped herself, ashamed that she'd even begun to ask.

"Two," she said, her gaze steady on Sadie's. "Before Graham."

The quiet pause that hovered between them felt ear-splitting. Klara's shoes squeaked from the other side of the exam door, but Johanna simply waited with an accepting look softening her features.

"It was my third," Sadie finally whispered. "Yesterday."

"Yesterday?" Johanna's hand found hers for another gripping squeeze. "I can't believe that you're working today. I couldn't get out of bed for several days after each of mine."

"I—I need the distraction . . ."

Johanna nodded as silence enveloped them for a few heartbeats.

"I'd tell you it's okay, but I know that it isn't. For me, each time felt like I was losing a part of myself. It was devastating." Her patient's voice filtered in through her blurry view of the bone anatomy posters across the exam room. "It's like my life as a before and an after. I was never the same after."

Johanna's words acted like a wrecking ball to the chiseled-down remnants of the concrete, steel-reinforced barrier surrounding Sadie's heart.

"I never expected it would be this hard." She wilted with an exhale. "It's *so* hard. Each time, I think, this will be it. This will be the person who completes our family, but when I lose them"—her voice cracked—"it's so excruciating."

"I know," Johanna whispered.

Sitting next to a woman who'd been where she was made her feel like the weight that had been sitting heavy on her spine lessened a tiny increment. She'd never spoken about her miscarriages, never really detailed how hard it had hit her—how each time she felt like she was being shattered from the inside.

Sadie wiped her nose. When her gaze dropped to her knees, she realized that Johanna's orthopedic boot was only halfway unfastened. She cleared her throat and swallowed hard before leaning to reach for the last two strips of black Velcro.

Johanna's hand on her shoulder stopped her. "I want to give you something." She leaned back and undid the clasp of the delicate gold chain behind her neck. "A friend of mine gave this to me after my second miscarriage. Neither of us are religious, and I think it's supposed to be for travelers, but"—she let out a little puff of air that was almost a chuckle—"I always felt like *this* was the reason for my boys. Like wearing it, I had this silent guardian protecting us."

She turned over Sadie's hand, and the warmed metal coiled into a small pile at the center. Within the small circular medallion, a man with a walking stick carried a child on his back.

"I can't—" She struggled. "And you haven't delivered. What if something goes wrong?"

Johanna's smile was warm. "This one's a tough guy, I can already tell, and I'm a scheduled C-section because Graham decided to wreck things on his way out last time." She closed Sadie's fingers around the necklace. "Take it."

Her gaze darted between her patient's eyes. "You're sure?"

Johanna nodded.

Sadie opened her hand again and then closed it around the necklace, slipping it into the pocket of her white coat. "Thank you."

A few minutes later, after she'd examined Johanna's foot and confirmed that, thankfully, she didn't need surgery, Sadie let herself into the single-use staff bathroom to collect herself. She pressed palms full of cold water over her red and puffy eyes. When she finally felt ready, she dug in her pocket for the necklace and ran her thumb over the picture pressed into the metal. A deep breath filled her as she clasped the chain around her neck, tucking the medallion beneath her shirt collar.

When she strode back into the busy hallway, Klara was waiting for her with another tablet. "Forty-eight year-old—"

"I need you to put the pro-bono code in Johanna's chart. Dr. Harvill shouldn't have sent her to me. I don't want her insurance charged for today." Even if Johanna had needed surgery, Sadie would have waived her surgeon's fee.

"Of course," the aide said before finishing the quick report on her next patient.

"Thank you." Sadie took the tablet from Klara before striding to the next exam room. As she raised her hand to the door, she paused, laying it instead over the pendant resting just above her heart. Her eyes fluttered closed. After another deep, settling breath, she knocked, moving on with the rest of her very busy day.

·CHAPTER 8·

Like usual, Clark got to Peaceably Park fifteen minutes before class to help Miles unload his truck. The former SEAL, now fitness trainer, creator, and owner of Dad Bod Fitness, hopped down from the driver's seat with a warm wave. The outdoor group fitness class was comprised solely of fathers and their stroller-secured children. When Clark had started attending class a few weeks after Lottie was born, Miles had brought his fraternal twins with him, but now that they were both in kindergarten, he taught the class solo.

"Mornin'."

"Hey." Clark opened the tailgate and reached in to grab the twenty, thirty, and forty-pound medicine balls.

They exchanged small talk while unloading the free weights, plates, and a large tire. Lottie sang a stumbly version of "The Itsy Bitsy Spider" from her spot strapped in the stroller.

Dad Bod Fitness gave Clark a routine and allowed him to get a good workout in, but he'd also gained an indispensable community. Having other fathers, most of whom were full-time, stay-at-home dads like him, to ask questions had given Clark a lifeline in the unpredictable and sometimes angry sea that was parenting.

No, still getting up every two hours at eight weeks wasn't unusual.

Yes, she'll drool more before she cuts her first tooth.

No, licking sand from her fingers while she plays in the sandbox wasn't weird for a nine-month-old.

Yes, it's okay on a really tough toddler day to let her eat goldfish crackers for breakfast, lunch, and dinner.

As much as he'd leaned on his community for the best way to prepare sweet potatoes for baby food or how to potty train, Clark's neck pinched thinking of how to broach the subject that weighed heavily on his mind this morning.

The rest of the regulars filed in over the next couple of minutes, parking their kids in a circle in the middle of the ramada so the older kids could socialize and the babies could see each other. Lottie squealed and grabbed the hand of her little friend Omar when his stroller was locked into place next to hers.

At nine o'clock, Miles announced, "Two laps around the perimeter of the park, and then we'll get to work."

Every dad was welcome at the class, and there were varied fitness levels in attendance. A few of them started walking and chatting with each other, and several others ran, but Clark settled into an easy jog, trying to let his mind clear. He hadn't slept much last night. Every time Sadie had moved in her sleep, he'd awoken. She'd gotten up earlier than normal to get to the office for her appointments today, and he'd lain in bed pretending to be asleep, listening to the sounds of her getting ready.

When she'd spent longer than usual in the shower, his heart had felt as if it was dissolving. The knowledge that she had probably been crying under the water—but if he'd walked into their bathroom he'd be unwelcome—had pressed all the air out of his body.

Clark pulled a hard breath into his lungs and focused on the picturesque park around him. The line of cherry trees along the paved running path had long since bloomed and now were brimming with new green leaves. Azalea bushes covered in pink, red, and white blossoms dotted the ground between their trunks. His eye caught on a groundswoman holding a watering can over three flowering plants in the mulch bed of a lone sweetgum maple along the edge of the park.

"What's up, Clark?" Jayce caught up and settled into pace beside him.

"Hey." He pulled his gaze to his friend's face.

"Miles said we're doing partner class today. Want to pair up?" Since they were close in physical strength and stamina, they usually did on partner workout days.

"Sounds good. How'd your game go?"

Jayce was in an amateur, but very intense, men's soccer league, and they'd had a game the night before. Listening to Jayce give a play-by-play, Clark felt his shoulders lower a fraction.

He let a little over half the class pass before he broached the subject that weighed heavily on his mind. "I want to ask you about something." Miles had separated all the stations at least twenty feet away from each other, but Clark still kept his voice down to prevent being overheard.

Clark chest passed the forty-pound medicine ball to his partner, mirroring the curtsy squat left and then right before preparing his hands to catch the ball again.

"Yeah?" The words came out with a grunt as Jayce passed the ball back.

The lump that had been near constant in this throat all morning felt as big as the ball in his hands as he swallowed over it. "Sadie miscarried yesterday."

Jayce's squat faltered, but he recovered quickly. "That sucks. I've been there. There's nothing worse. I'm sorry." He caught the ball. "Are you okay?"

It was the first time someone had asked him that, and Clark had to grit his teeth hard to keep the liquid threatening at the edge of his vision from joining the sweat on his face.

"Yeah. I'm all right," he lied.

They moved in silence for a few rounds before he continued, "I just . . . she won't talk to me about it, and I don't know how to make things better. It seems like whatever I do is always the wrong thing."

"Give her some time. It just happened. It can be really jarring."

The ball passed two times before he could bring himself to tell the truth. "It was her third."

"Oh." His partner's eyes softened. "Oh, man." He blew out a breath. "Did you guys—"

"See the specialist? Yeah, after the second one. We got all the testing done, and everything seems normal, but this keeps happening."

Jayce tsked. "Well, she'll still need time. I know with Caroline, she kinda went into a fog for a week after hers."

Miles blew the whistle to switch stations, and they moved on to dumbbell thrusters.

"Did she ever . . ." The words caught in Clark's throat, but he forced them out. "Shut down on you?"

"No. Caroline was kind of the opposite. I felt like she wanted to hash it out constantly, and I ended up being the one who needed to take a break from talking about it." He paused, pushing the weights high over his head. "Whatever you do, don't try to fix it. I made that mistake."

Clark winced. Was suggesting adoption trying to "fix things?" Maybe that was why she'd been so angry every time he'd brought it up.

He just wanted Lottie to have a sibling. He loved his parents and was incredibly grateful that he had a close relationship with them, but growing up, he'd always felt so alone. If he hadn't been at school, he'd been by himself, usually scrounging around the woods for hours. When he'd grown tired of that, he'd quietly sat and read at his father's side as he'd worked on his latest novel. Clark didn't want Lottie to grow up feeling the same emptiness he'd always known.

"What'd you do?" His friend's voice brought him back to the park.

When he looked up, Jayce had stopped his set.

"Are we talking, or are we working?" Miles called out from his position in the center of the strollers, blowing bubbles toward the kids.

They both continued in silence for a few beats before Clark asked, "Is it 'fixing things' to bring up other options for having a child?"

Jayce thought for a moment. "Not necessarily. There was a point when we were considering adoption, but then the pregnancy with Grace stuck."

The whistle tweeted.

"Okay," he said, moving to the next station. They both got into plank position and started alternating reach out high-fives. "But she gets really angry when I bring it up."

"Did you bring it up yesterday?"

Clark stared at the black mat under his hands and swore.

"Don't be so hard on yourself," Jayce said. "It's not like there's an instruction manual for this or anything. Though Caroline would joke that if there was one, I wouldn't have read it anyway."

Clark laughed for what felt like the first time in weeks, his abs straining from the action while being in plank. "I'm actually pretty good at reading instructions."

"Well, la-di-da." Jayce slapped his hand.

They continued until Miles blew three quick tweets letting them know that stations were over, and it was time for a concentrated ab circuit before cool down.

"The biggest advice I can offer is just to be there for her. Silence is okay. If she ends up talking, just listen." They laid on their backs per Mile's instructions to start bicycles. "And I'm sure Sadie knows this because she's a doctor, but make sure you tell her it isn't her fault. That she's not broken. Something like one in four pregnancies ends in miscarriage, but nobody ever tells you that because no one ever talks about it. Caroline thought it was something she was doing wrong, but that's just not how it works. I still remember the look on her face when I told her it wasn't her. It was like watching this heavy weight lift off her body."

"I did say that." He'd at least gotten one thing right last night.

"Good."

Miles called out to them again, and they switched to leg raises.

"And give yourself time to feel sad about it yourself. It's not just her loss, it's yours as well. You can always talk to me if you need to," Jayce added.

"Thanks." That small, simple acknowledgement assuaged the maelstrom of emotions tugging at his weary muscles.

Jayce let them finish the rest of the abs circuit and the stretching afterward in silence. They rolled the mats and tucked them under their arms before grabbing a few dumbbells to carry to Miles's truck. After all the dads had picked up the equipment, Jayce's hand stopped Clark's shoulder on the way to the strollers.

"One more thing," he said quietly as the rest of the dads moved toward the kids. "You guys can't try again for a few weeks anyway, so I'd focus on reconnecting right now. Caroline and I tried to do some more date nights, and though the first few right after were awkward, I felt like when we decided to go for it again, we were back on the same page. Then Grace was conceived, and it all"—he looked off to the trees and blew out a breath—"don't mock me, but it felt like it was meant to be."

Clark nodded with understanding. When Sadie had stepped out of his apartment bathroom more than three years ago and blurted out that she was pregnant, it had seemed like some large cosmic hand had just given him the best gift of his life. He'd already been mind-blowingly in love with her, ready to propose to her, and now she was carrying his child. It was simply too perfect.

"Good advice." He cleared his throat. "You staying to let Grace play?"

Jayce's daughter was a year younger than Lottie, but she often toddled after his daughter on the playground following class.

"We've got to jet off to her eighteen-month well check for S-H-O-T-S." He spelled the offending word, now that they were in earshot of the preschool-age kids.

Clark wrinkled his nose. "Good luck."

Jayce laughed without humor. "I'll need it. Holding them down for that is the worst." He steered his stroller to the parking lot.

Clark wanted to disengage his stroller break and head to his truck himself, but he knew if he did, his only company would be his daughter for the rest of the day. Usually, he had some afternoon activity for Lottie—library story time or swimming lessons, but today's schedule was vacant.

"Did you see the Giants and the Reds last night?" Victor, Omar's dad, asked.

"I missed it. Any good?"

Victor bounced with a groan and proceeded to provide Clark with just the distraction he needed as they wheeled their kids to the nearby playground.

·CHAPTER 9·

Hook keys. Flats off. Sadie moved through her getting home routine like she'd been moving through the last two weeks, on autopilot. It had been almost impossible to hide the hollowed feeling that constantly cloaked her skin from her colleagues. Unfortunately, Josh had had his appointments in the office with her today. After he'd spent the moments between their respective patients critiquing her most recent director decision over staffing and coordination with the hospital's surgical nurses, he'd offered to take over her last two appointments with a false smile, stating she "looked exhausted."

Though most of the surgeons in their group worked as a team and generally supported each other, Josh was that prototypical arrogant surgeon who thought that he was more skilled than everyone else, particularly her. A little over a year ago, she'd been almost unanimously selected to be the new director—except for one vote. It hadn't been challenging to determine who the one "nay" had been.

Sadie sighed, running her hand over her ponytail before an object beneath her feet stopped her evening flow. A scuffed pair of women's white Pumas carelessly littered the entry mat. Sadie groaned as her body sagged with fatigue, remembering that Clark had scheduled a date night for them. Aurelia, their college-age sitter, was already here. She must have parked beside the woodshop where Sadie would have missed her car.

Stepping over the shoes, Sadie continued toward the study to drop off her messenger bag. Clark was sitting on the stairs and rose as she came by.

"Hey." The boyish hope in his eyes sliced through her like a scalpel. "I called Stove and pushed our reservation back. You don't have to change if you don't want to."

Her eyes fell over her traditional office day attire—slacks and a collared shirt—before taking in that Clark was wearing the slate-blue cashmere sweater she'd bought him for Christmas, even though it'd been eighty degrees today. He also had on grey slacks she hadn't seen before and the black dress shoes he'd worn at their wedding.

Her brain warred with her. He clearly was trying to make an effort—Clark usually lived in jeans and T-shirts or exercise clothes—but she was already mentally and physically exhausted. Having to sit across from his beautiful face and watch it twist in disappointment during a gourmet meal sounded as appealing as another phone call with her mother.

Penelope's words from her requisite bi-monthly call on the drive home still rang in Sadie's ears. She'd always suspected the entire purpose of their conversations was for her mother to flaunt her superiority. If it hadn't disappointed her father when she hadn't answered her mother's calls, Sadie wouldn't have kept enduring them.

"*Family's blood, Sadie girl.*" The memory of his scratchy voice still resounded.

Tonight's call hadn't been anything new; it was always the same onslaught of grievances. Sadie was too soft—her mother's way of saying not thin enough. Sadie was too plain—she should do something with her hair, her makeup, her nails. It was distasteful that she had a man's job and that her husband was raising their child. In essence, Sadie wasn't *woman* enough.

With Mother's Day looming three days away, Sadie was already struggling with the feelings of imposter syndrome following her third miscarriage and second-guessing every decision she'd made about her daughter.

And since Penelope had been in a particularly ruthless mood tonight, she'd laid the largest charge before the call disconnected—that she didn't know how a handsome man like Clark put up with Sadie.

Sadie opened her mouth, but nothing came out. In that action, the light died in her husband's eyes.

"She's already here, putting Lottie to bed." He gestured up the stairs.

She wanted to explain that it wasn't about Aurelia. It was if they went out to eat and she didn't talk enough, or have the right amount of fun, or not kiss him the right way at the end of the night, she'd end up letting him down again. She'd already let him down three devastating times, but if she could conceive again and keep this baby, maybe Clark would love her the way he used to.

Her fingertips pressed the placket of her black shirt, feeling for the metal circle beneath. Though she'd never taken her new necklace off, the scientific-minded side of her brain—the side that had prevailed for decades—kept whispering that it was just inert metal, not a magical charm. Still, she couldn't help but hope.

"I'm just not up for dinner out." The defeated look on his face shredded her insides. "We can spend time together. I'd just like to be at home."

His jaw loosened. "All right. I'm going to pay her for the full night anyway."

"Of course."

"We can watch a movie or something."

She nodded before heading up the stairs to their bedroom. Sadie took her time in their en suite bathroom brushing her hair out of its ponytail, listening for Aurelia's exit. She slipped out of her work clothes, her eyes lingering on her softened belly. When she grazed her skin, pain rocketed from the pads of her fingers up her forearms. A sharp breath filled her lungs, and she focused while exhaling it evenly. Pulling her shoulders into their locked position, she slipped one of her old silk nightshirts over her underwear.

"What movie do you want to wa—" Clark's question died on his tongue.

"Hey," she was going for sexy, but her voice game out slightly strained.

Her husband's lips pressed into a firm line. "You're going to be a little cold watching a movie in that. I turned the AC on today."

She attempted an alluring shrug. "Or we can stay up here."

Clark pinched the bridge of his nose before rubbing his hand over his face. His breath was as audible as it was long. "No, Sadie."

"No?" Though technically everything was covered, she suddenly felt embarrassingly naked.

His expression was softer when he lifted his face. "Let's have some cereal and watch one of those obstacle reality shows you love while we snuggle on the couch."

That offer sounded like heaven, better than reconstructing a comminuted pelvis—her favorite surgery. It sounded like something the old Clark and Sadie would have done before falling asleep in each other's arms. But the fact that she could probably conceive again weighed too heavily on her mind.

She let her left shoulder droop, knowing the thin strap would fall off with that action. Clark's eyes snagged at the bare open space no longer covered by lavender-dyed silk and followed the line down to her breasts. He blinked twice before turning to leave the bathroom, tossing his words over his shoulder.

"I bought more Cap'n Crunch today."

"Wait," she lunged forward, grabbing his wrist. That electric pulse that sometimes accompanied touching Clark surged up her arm. "Don't you want. . . ." She let the question drop off.

A hoarse exhale preceded his hands framing her face, ensuring her gaze was fixed on his. "I do. More than you can imagine." He swallowed hard, loosening his grip a bit. "But I think what would be best for us right now would be cereal and watching unnecessarily fit people doing crazy stunts."

She opened her mouth to protest.

"Maybe one of them will accidentally make a mistake and break something in a gruesome way, and you can tell me how you'd fix it." His voice was attempting to be light, but there was no humor in his eyes as they darted between hers.

"But—"

He let go of her face, stepping back and slamming an open hand against the wall. "Damn it, Sadie. I'm not a sperm factory."

Sadie jumped at the sound of his palm slapping the plaster. He'd never done anything like that before.

"I—" She shook her head rapidly. "I never said—"

"You don't have to." His hand fisted the air at his side. "That's all you want me for. Do you know how long it's been since you've initiated touch with me? *Seven days*." The last words were growled through closed teeth.

"It's been seven days since I leaned in for a goodbye kiss and got a peck in return. But tonight, you're wearing that and reaching out for me, and I know it's not because you want *me*." The anger in his eyes washed away, leaving breath-halting sadness in its wake. "Because I've been here all week. I'm *always* right here."

Her stomach squeezed and twisted in an excruciating way. "Clark, I—"

He held up a hand and backed away. "I can't. I just—I'm going for a drive."

Slippery silk met her fingertips before she realized she was hugging herself. The sound of each of Clark's footfalls as they marched away from her was agony, the jingle of his truck keys a punch in the face. The finality of the garage door closing set off a silence within their large house that Sadie immediately wanted to cover with something. Impulsively, she flicked on the tap. Liquid flowed down the sink in blatant disregard for water conservation as she tried to catch her breath.

It was over. It had to be over.

She'd never seen him like that. He'd *never* walked out on her before.

The truth sat heavy at the base of her spine.

Her time with him was up.

Sadie knew she should be grateful that she'd had nearly four years with Clark, but pervasive achiness was the only thing that registered. More numbly than before, she moved through her bedtime routine and changed into her usual cotton tank and shorts pajama set. Though she turned off the light and pretended to be asleep, it wasn't until hours later when the garage opened that some of the tightness in her quads loosened.

But then Clark never came upstairs, and she knew with certainty that the tiny sliver of hope she'd be gripping had shattered in a way she couldn't pin or screw it back together.

·CHAPTER 10·

"You wanted to talk to me?" In front of her scrubs, Sadie held the bright orange sticky note that he'd hung over her mirror. The black marker letters stated: *We have to talk. I'm in the woodshop.* Aimlessly driving around town last night, Clark had done a lot of thinking and come up with a plan.

Until hearing her voice, he'd still been pissed at Sadie. But now as the twilight sky silhouetted her body and the last of the sun's embers haloed her auburn ponytail, he resisted the overwhelming urge to gather her in his arms. His wife was not standing in the doorway to his woodshop—some broken woman was. He'd never seen Sadie look so small, and he hated the sight of it.

Powering off his saw, he cleared his throat. "I wanted to let you know that I scheduled us another date night. For Sunday."

Her auburn brows pinched. "But . . . why?"

Clark wanted to shout, *To save our marriage*, but instead, a deep, mournful part of him simply sighed. He didn't know how to get from being twenty feet away, tersely talking to his wife, to where they'd been before they tried to give Lottie a sibling.

"I did a lot of thinking last night." Her eyes darted down at his words, and he had to tighten his calves to prevent him from crossing the room. "And I realized we never really dated."

Since the moment they'd met, they'd always had this insatiable need for each other. And because of her schedule, they'd spent those first few months before she'd found out she was pregnant in each other's homes, usually half-naked. After that, it had been a blur of getting ready for a wedding, buying a house, and the mind-jolting reality that was parenting.

"Halloween happened and then. . . ." He let his sentence drop off as the familiar memory played automatically.

Clark surveyed half of the crowded living room before his eyes snagged on her.

Damned if he didn't have a thing for redheads. Especially a redhead with curves straining the pale green fabric of her sexy surgeon costume. Technically, she was covered from head to toe in what looked like regular scrubs, complete with a surgical cap tied around her head, but on her, they looked incredible.

He was cutting through the room when a half-dressed zombie with extensive tattoos pressed a red cup into her hand. The zombie whispered something in her ear before continuing to pass three more cups to others.

"Hey." His grin rose when he arrived before her.

She didn't answer, but the smile on her lips hit his stomach with the force of a nail gun.

"I'm Clark," he said, outstretching his hand.

"Clark. Right." *She extended the word as her eyes flowed over his black rimmed costume glasses, his open collared white dress shirt with a Superman T-shirt beneath, and belted black jeans. He'd even taken a strand of his hair and curled it over his forehead with a little pomade.*

When her gaze flicked back to his face, a flash of what looked like uncertainty skirted across it. She took a deep breath before tossing back the entire contents of her cup in one large gulp.

"Sadie," she said, setting the plastic cup on the fireplace mantel beside them and taking his hand.

Clark had seen enough rom-com movies over the years to have witnessed the portrayal of the spark when lovers first touch, and he'd often rolled his eyes watching that scene play out. But when Sadie slid her hand into his, it felt like the time an electrician on the job had left a live wire open and he'd brushed against it.

The stunned cough that came out of his mouth was as unintentional as it was slightly embarrassing. Sadie let go, wiggling her fingers as they returned to her side.

She lifted her chin, tilted her head an inch, and then said with the self-possession of someone who was used to giving orders, "Follow me."

Clark fell into step behind her as she wove around the makeshift living room dance floor, through the kitchen, and down the entry hallway. An entertained smirk laced his lips as he followed her into the unoccupied garage before she turned and shoved him against the closed door.

Before he could take a breath, her lips were on his, the taste of fresh squeezed lemon juice and gin lingering on her tongue as it teased its way into his mouth. Those wiggly fingers gripped the sides of his face with a determined firmness.

His response was as enthusiastic as it was instinctual. He chased her tongue with his, ran his hands down her sides to grip her waist tightly, and pulled their bodies flush against each other. A throaty puff of air escaped her in response. Then her hands were just as wild as they dove into his hair, knocking his glasses to the ground.

"Sorry." She started to crouch to pick them up, and he stopped her with a hand against her ribcage.

"It's okay. They're fake."

That shyness played at her features again. At this proximity, he noticed her eyes matched the pale green of her scrubs.

"I don't usually do things like this, but Parker said I should get out of my own way."

Whoever this Parker was, he'd have to thank them later.

"I'm not complaining." He let a devilish smile accompany his words as his thumb played with her lowest rib.

Her eyes widened slightly before they fell to his mouth again, and that was all it took. Lips and tongues and hands played as the strong bassline thrummed on the opposite side of the door. The vibrations of the music pulsed through the wood barrier into his spine.

She looked down, fisting his shirts in her right hand and bringing their edges up over his waistband. This incredible half-hum/half-grunt came out of her mouth, and he was absolutely certain he'd never heard a sexier noise.

"You have my favorite feature." Her fingertips tickled the skin over the angled groove peeking over his belt. "Colloquially, it's called an Adonis belt, but it's actually made of the inguinal ligament and the transverse abdominis."

Clark tightened his abs and tilted his hip so her fingers would get lost deeper in the groove, and that same sound ripped free from her throat again.

His hand roughly found the edge of her jaw, tilting it up and capturing her lips in another drugging kiss. "Tell me you live nearby."

The smile that curled her mouth made everything in him clench. "Right across the complex."

"Perfect," he rasped, a second before he crushed his mouth to the crook of her neck.

Clark had never felt that kind of immediate connection with a woman before. It had been jarring as much as it had been addicting. After that point, he'd taken as much of Sadie as he could get.

His wife seemed to be lost in the same memory as the back of her index finger traced the part of her neck that he'd sucked on years ago. That single simple action almost made him want to throw this whole plan out the window.

He swallowed hard, organizing his thoughts. "Everything has always been such a whirlwind. Maybe we should take the time now. I'd like to take you out. Bring you flowers. The whole nine yards."

"You've gotten me flowers before."

He ran a sawdust-covered hand over his face. "Love, you're not listening to me. I want to take things slow. I want us to spend time together that isn't wrapped up in parenting or trying to achieve a goal." He knew that statement would cause her to bristle, but it needed to be said.

Sadie stood silently for several beats until she quickly twisted her wrist—her tell for when she was nervous about something.

The gesture made his chest ache. Maybe he wasn't alone in this. Maybe she was as anxious as he was about the degradation of their relationship.

Her answer came out as a single breathy word. "Okay."

"One more thing," he began, carefully watching her expression. "No sex."

Her lips tensed, but she kept herself from frowning.

"The point of us dating is to spend time together for the sake of it." And hopefully for them to find a way to reconnect. "I don't want to blur any lines."

Her jaw worked, but she stayed silent. Instead, she gave him a single curt nod.

"I know it's Mother's Day, so I thought we'd keep it easy— dinner and a movie."

Sadie took a deep breath before she finally said, "Fine."

He waited for her to say more, but in the end, she claimed she had charts to finish and then strode back into the night air.

Clark waited to turn his saw back on. He needed his heart to slow down and his hands to stop shaking so that he wouldn't accidentally lose any fingers. Instead, the tips of them cradled his forehead as he let out a resigned exhale. She'd said yes, he should be pleased, but the way she'd resisted had cut through him like a diamond-bladed circular saw.

Time.

This was going to take time. It'd taken them a year to get here, and it was going to take time to get back. As he flipped the machine back on and continued to cut perfect forty-five degree angles, he hoped that it wasn't too late.

·CHAPTER 11·

As it turns out, Sadie never got to have a date night with her husband on Mother's Day because at two in the afternoon, she was jolted from sleep by Clark calling her, slightly panicked, from the pediatric dentist's office. Though she'd technically gotten eight hours of sleep since she'd crawled into bed after her long call night at six a.m.—thirty minutes before Clark's alarm—sleeping during the day always made her disoriented.

Since southern summer had already arrived, she'd thrown on a pair of shorts and a T-shirt, shoved her feet into sandals, and was racing to the location Clark texted her before realizing she'd never gone to the bathroom or brushed her teeth. Sadie hadn't been to the pediatric dentist's office, but the building held the same beige squat architecture common of medical offices.

Pulling into the empty parking lot next to Clark's slate grey truck, an unexpected nervousness swept through her. She shook it off, straightened her frame, and strode into the office like it was her own OR.

It only took a few moments of talking with the warm Dr. Ramirez, who had her husband and adorable six-month-old daughter with her, to understand the medical aspects of what Clark had told her on the phone. Lottie had smashed her alveolar process when she'd fallen face-first into the park playground stairs.

"Fortunately, there's no mandibular fracture, but the teeth are very loose. I know a lot of parents are wary of sedation, particularly with the littles, but I really think if I can get a quick suture around each affected tooth, it'll increase the chances that she'll keep them. They're going to yellow from the trauma, but they should be able to function. Then she won't have a gap until she's five and the permanent teeth come in." The doctor twisted her lips to the side. "With her being a finger sucker, I'm doubtful they'll stay in on their own."

A tearful Lottie was in Clark's lap, distraught because it was nap time and she couldn't suck on her hand, rubbing her face into his sternum.

Normally, Sadie would have just answered. In the past, whenever anything medical came up with their daughter, Clark had always yielded to her. But with the way things had been between them, she paused and waited until she caught Clark's eye. "I think we should do it. What do you think?"

His dark lashes fluttered. "Uh . . . yeah. I mean, I'm worried, but we'll be right there, right?" His gaze flicked to the dentist's.

Dr. Ramirez smiled at him. "You can hold her hand the whole time."

Clark nodded, his hands gripping Lottie closer to him before his gaze returned to Sadie's. "All right."

Her husband ended up holding Lottie's left hand as his other hand rested on their daughter's chest. Sadie knew the placement was to calm Lottie at first, but the diligent way Clark watched their daughter's tiny ribs rise and fall told her that it was also to soothe his own fears. Sadie's body swelled with emotion as she reached across the dentist chair to grip his hand over their daughter's heart. Her husband looked surprised at the touch, but the tight lines in his forehead loosened as their gazes held.

In the end, Lottie did well with the laughing gas, and the dentist only needed to suture three of the bottom front teeth.

"I know that the AAP *and* the AAPD have a hard stance on juice, but dental sutures can sometimes give off a bad taste until they dissolve. If she's complaining of something yucky over the next five days, let her have some of her favorite juice to wash out the taste." Dr. Rameriz winked at Lottie before quickly reviewing the recommended soft diet.

Though their daughter had been fully revived to assure that all her reflexes were intact prior to leaving, she lasted the length of the parking lot before she passed out on Clark's shoulder.

"Should you come with us?" he asked, gingerly buckling their sleeping daughter into her car seat. "What if something happens when I'm driving, and I can't get to her?"

The surgeon part of her wanted to explain that the half-life of nitrous oxide was five minutes and they'd spent more than ten minutes talking to the dentist after Lottie had already returned to consciousness. When Clark finished the last buckle, his strong fingers found and gripped the base of his neck, and that same emotional swell overtook her.

"I'll come home with you and then order a car to drive me back here."

His eyes darted to hers. "You're sure?"

"Yeah."

When they arrived home, Lottie was awake and angry that her mouth hurt. Clark gave her liquid ibuprofen and acetaminophen and made her a fruit smoothie without a straw. Sadie ordered the car and canceled Aurelia before getting her RAV4 from the dentist's office.

Clark and Lottie weren't in their daughter's bathroom when she got home but instead were in the master shower. Lottie's giggle bounced off the fogged mirror, arrowing for Sadie's heart. Behind the glass shower door, Clark had their daughter on his swim trunk covered hip as she held her hands aloft.

"Oh, no no no. *Lottie.* Don't you dare. Don't you—"

Their daughter brought her hands down on his head, billows of shaving cream squashing between her little fingers into Clark's dark, wet hair.

He blew the errant puffs of cream out of his face with a mock gasp. "I can't believe you did that. Now, I have to give you raspberries."

Grasping her forearm, he blew hard on her slick upper arm. The adorable squeal that followed had Sadie's feet marching to the door and pulling it open.

"What is going on here?" she asked with pretend exasperation.

It took Clark a breath to realize that she was trying to play too.

"This one did it." He pointed to their daughter. "This one, officer, take her away."

"No, Dada," Lottie laughed.

"Hmm." Sadie tapped her finger on her chin before reaching into the shower to grab the canister of shaving cream. "Is this the offending weapon?"

"Yeah!" Lottie clapped her wet hands together.

Before Clark could come up with another jokey response, she covered her palm with cream and smeared it over his entire face. When he held very still for two long seconds, Sadie's heart pounded in her ears. She'd just been trying to play along with them. It'd been so long since they'd all been like this, maybe she'd done it wrong. Her shaky hands set the canister back on the built-in tiled nook.

Then he blew out his breath, covering her teal T-shirt with dots of cream. "That's it. Lottie, you're on my team now. Operation Get Mommy!"

He'd rinsed his face and set down and armed Lottie before Sadie could register that she hadn't disappointed him. In fact, a playful, evil gleam settled in his eyes as he covered his own palms. Lottie smeared her exposed calves and shins with cream, pulling a deep laugh from Sadie's belly. When she looked up to find her husband's lit eyes already focused on her face, her breath sat trapped in her chest.

"I always thought you'd look lovely with a beard." His hand cupped one cheek and then the other so delicately she wanted to lean into his palm despite the shaving cream.

"More!" Lottie bounced and then slipped. As her wet little bottom hit the river rock floor of their shower, she burst into tears.

"Okay, no more shaving cream." Clark swooped her up and started rinsing them both off. "Love, do you want to shower?" When he glanced at her, it felt like the past year hadn't happened. The tone, the inflection, the ease at which the sentence tumbled off his tongue. It was as if all that pain had never occurred.

But then she remembered it had. She remembered loss after loss and pulled her gaze away. "No, I'll just wipe it off with a towel."

Sadie left the bathroom to put her shaving cream-covered towel in the laundry room sink and let herself continue down the stairs. She didn't understand what she was doing until her bare feet crossed the dewy evening grass to the playhouse. Sunset light streamed through the compact glass windows Clark had installed, though most of them were left open all the time. He'd built little shelves and tucked a plastic play kitchen into a corner. Sadie didn't recognize the handmade kid's wooden table and chair set placed near it.

She tugged the hair tie from her ponytail and backed up until she slid down the chalkboard wall. Later she'd explain away the chalk dust on the back of her T-shirt, but now she needed to remember to breathe. Her arms wrapped around her knees as she pulled the humid air into her lungs.

"You get five minutes. Five minutes, then you need to do bedtime tonight. She's had a hard day," Sadie whispered.

She'd been doing this a lot over the last several months. Sometimes, she'd get up, put on scrubs as if she was going to surgery, and then sit on top of a picnic table at a park at sunrise, just like this. Other times, she'd find refuge in various single-use bathrooms on different floors of the hospital. Every time curled into a ball, knowing that she needed to process the heartache pitted deep in her body, but also aware she didn't know how.

When her heart rate slowed, she rose from her position, pulled her hair up, and returned to the house. Clark was already singing, so she silently slid into Lottie's bedroom. After hearing their daughter's breathy slumber, they moved through the rest of the things that needed to be done—cleaning up and feeding themselves something.

The sidelong glances that came her way became too much after a while, so she sat herself at her computer, catching up on the charting from the mass casualty highway accident that had kept her at the hospital until nearly daylight. As she usually did when she worked, she lost track of time. Only the sound of the TV turning off and then Clark climbing the stairs alerted her to the fact that it was nearly ten.

She waited another five minutes, shuffling around the clutter on her desk, before heading upstairs to get ready for bed. When she walked out of the bathroom, Clark was awake instead of asleep with the light off, like normal. His eyes were on the ceiling, one hand over his heart, the other behind his head. Her bedside sconce was on, though his was off.

After tucking herself under the covers, she reached to turn off her light.

"Thank you." His whispered words were barely audible.

Abandoning the sconce, she turned in bed to face her husband. He didn't move from his position, his strong jaw evident as it tilted skyward. Part of her wanted to clarify what he was thanking her for, but then this serene look washed over his face as his eyelashes rested on his cheek. Breath after even breath raised and lowered his bare chest.

Sadie knew he wasn't asleep, but Clark seemed more relaxed that she'd seen him in months. She almost didn't want to move for fear she'd disturb him. In the end, she reached in slow degrees until her fingertips touched the metal, turning the light off. Instead of settling into her normal position, she stacked her hands under her pillow and pulled her top leg toward the center of the bed.

"Goodnight," she murmured almost silently in case he was already sleeping.

As the Benadryl she'd taken to help her readjust to normal sleep hours pulled at her last threads of consciousness, she thought she heard "Goodnight, love" whispered in return.

·CHAPTER 12·

Lottie scribbled half-on/half-off the yellow construction paper he'd set on her kid-sized wooden table behind the rectangular folding table which showcased his pieces at the Northwood Farmer's Market. Though it'd been a week since her dental procedure, a box of apple juice sat just beyond her elbow. Since she was behaving nicely this morning and allowing him to talk to customers as they meandered by, Clark felt she deserved it.

He moved around the front of the display table to replace the three-foot by eighteen-inch panel he'd just sold with another piece. His larger pieces were propped between the asphalt and the top edge of the table, and he'd built a few display blocks for the smaller twelve-by-twelve pieces. Last week, a customer had asked for a business card, and he'd been embarrassed to say he didn't have one. This week, a handmade wooden holder held slim pieces of card stock touting "Clark Benson, Woodsmith" followed by his email.

"How's business?" Thatcher's wide frame blocked the sunlight streaming between canopy tents.

"You know what? Not bad. Each weekend, I sell more than the one prior." This was his fourth week, and Clark felt he'd finally gotten the flow of being on this side of the tent. "Hey, do you have a website?"

Robin had dropped by last week, sneaking Lottie an organic agave lollipop and mentioning that she did almost all of her business online through her website or various craft websites but liked the milieu of the farmer's market. That was why she'd coordinated with the town's leadership to start it in the first place.

Thatcher smoothed a hand over his thick beard. "I do, but I use it more to take orders for custom pieces and advertise what markets I'll be at."

"All right." He nodded to himself, pushing some sweat from his brow. The air was already sticky and warm, even though it was only midmorning. "Maybe I'll look into getting one this week."

"They're pretty easy now, with drag and drop builders." A throaty laugh punched from his belly. "If I can do it, you'll have no problem."

This hobby, which at first had been something to distract his brain during the long evening hours alone, now seemed like a tangible thing that he could push into something more if he really wanted to. An effervescent sensation rolled over his muscles, leaving possibility shining in its wake.

"I've got to get back. Just wanted to say hi." Thatcher waved and made his way back to his location mid-market.

Because Clark had started after the season had already begun, he was at the very end, but people still seemed to find him. Also, there were long stretches between customers where he could play with Lottie to keep her happy.

Coming to stand over Lottie's shoulder, he saw her three-circle drawing. Each crude circle had filled in oval eyes and a swoopy mouth. She grinned up at him before pointing at each circle.

"Dada. Ottie. Mama."

"I see that, little love. That looks just like us."

His chest squeezed thinking over the last week. After the connection they'd had after Lottie's accident, some foolhardy part of him had thought things would change. But Sadie was still working ridiculously long hours, and he was keeping everything going at home while whittling away in the woodshop during Lottie's nap or at night. Their communication hadn't improved.

Only one thing was different.

Now each night when Sadie slept, she faced him in bed.

Yesterday morning when he'd woken up to get Lottie ready before Dad Bod Fitness, Sadie had continued sleeping, having been at the hospital late the night before. Though the blackout curtains were snug over their bedroom windows, enough light had escaped them to reveal his wife's leg slung on top of the covers and her arm outstretched toward his side of the bed. He'd stood, simply watching her for a minute, his heart light because in her sleep, she'd reached for him.

Tonight, they were supposed to make up for last week's cancelled date, and he'd been more nervous thinking about dinner with his wife than he'd been about any date he'd ever been on. Lately, his stack of non-fiction books had transformed from his usual subjects of history, crime, and politics to the psychological variety. Though he'd had to keep the ones about reconnecting with your spouse and rebuilding a broken relationship hidden in his bedside drawer when Sadie was home.

"I think so too. But what about that one?" A young couple talking to themselves drew his attention back to the present.

Clark had learned it was better to wait until people addressed him rather than interjecting himself into their conversations, asking if they had questions. Plus, he could learn people's organic opinions of his work if he let them converse freely. That, and which designs he sold the most, helped him decide what to create next. He already had several ideas to try out while Lottie took her two-hour nap this afternoon.

Twenty minutes later, he'd cashed the young couple out after they'd purchased three of the twelve-by-twelve pieces to hang over their couch.

He pulled his phone from his front shorts pocket, checking the time. "It's almost closing time. Do you want to get a quesadilla from the food truck before we go home?" He swung his daughter up on his hip.

"Yeah!" she cheered, hugging his neck.

A smile tugged his lips taut before they turned down again. He was doing his best making a new schedule for him and Lottie, finding unexpected joy in creating something different and selling it among newfound friends, but he still missed what this day used to be.

Sundays used to be Sadie's only expected day at home. Monday through Friday she'd have scheduled surgeries and office hours. Occasionally, a call shift would pepper in throughout her schedule throwing her hours out of whack, forcing her to stay overnight at the hospital.

Sunday used to be their family day. A day that often involved a leisurely and messy pancake breakfast in their kitchen, followed by playtime in the backyard, or an occasional stroll through the farmer's market. They usually had lunch out together—trying the various eclectic restaurants in Northwood—before putting Lottie down for her nap and having "adult nap time." While he made dinner later, Sadie would have some solo playtime with Lottie.

But over the last few months, Sadie had started having scheduled Saturday surgeries or call shifts over both weekend days. The loss of the one day a week when he'd felt everything was perfect sat like a cinder block in his stomach.

Part of him suspected that his wife was picking up extra call shifts to keep herself busy. There was nothing Sadie liked more than surgery, and he expected being fist-deep into someone's body cavity had a tendency to keep one's focus off issues at home. But it still hurt.

No, that was a drastic understatement.

It shredded his insides that she'd rather be anywhere than in his presence—than in their daughter's presence.

"Would you take one-twenty for this?"

Clark's head shook, bringing him back to the market. A tiny elderly woman stood on the other side of his folding table, struggling to hold a three by eighteen panel of wood aloft with her thin, crepe-skinned arms.

His hand instinctively jutted out, bracing the wood piece before it smashed her on the head. "Only if you let me carry it to your car for you."

The woman's fingers released their hold on the wood to fluff her tight white curls before straightening the single strand of pearls over her high-collared blouse. "If you insist."

He couldn't help the broad smile on his face. "I insist."

◊◊◊

Clark rolled the ice ball around in his glass. He wasn't much of a drinker, but tonight, having a whiskey while he waited for his wife seemed appropriate. When she'd texted saying that things were running long in a meeting with the residency chair but she'd meet him at the restaurant, part of him had worried that she wouldn't show. He tried to shake off the thought, pushing a breath out of his nose while bringing the highball glass to his lips.

"Is this seat taken?" Sadie's soft words entered his ears as whiskey entered his mouth.

When he turned, he immediately choked—half-coughing/half-wheezing—as burning liquid went down the wrong pipe. He slapped his chest as he continued to hack, but managed a hoarse, "Sweet Jesus."

She firmly patted his back. "Sorry. I didn't mean to startle you."

The bartender pushed a glass of ice water in front of him, and Clark held up a hand to his wife, taking down gulps of cold water until his throat cleared and his eyes stopped watering.

"You didn't startle me." His words were still gravely from his burned throat. "I've just never—I mean where did you—" He stopped and took a deep breath to center himself. "You're wearing a dress."

The only time he'd seen Sadie in a dress had been at their wedding, and he'd gotten the distinct impression that the simple yet elegant vintage dress she'd picked out was to appease her mother more than something she'd been dreaming about since she was seven.

His wife looked down at herself and grimaced slightly. "It was Parker's suggestion."

Thank God for Parker.

With her gaze downcast, Clark stole the moment to let his eyes linger. The glimpse of her when she'd arrived had been enough to completely shock him, but now raw excitement ran through him that he was going to be able to stare at her for the rest of the night.

The deep blue, jewel-toned color of the sleeveless dress highlighted her pale skin and fiery hair. As nice as that was, it was how the dress tightly hugged her body from the shoulder until just over her knee that'd made him inhale liquor. Thick straps wove down into a rounded neckline that ended in a sharp V. It was nearly impossible for his eyes not to fixate there. He'd never seen his wife's cleavage showcased in such a way. The impulse to ask her to turn around so he could see his favorite part of her singed his tongue.

Her head lifted, and he forced his to do the same. On the way back up, he noticed a small pendant necklace decorating her skin. Sadie rarely wore jewelry. The engagement ring he'd given her sat in a small box in their closet most of the time, though she never took off her rose gold wedding band.

"Is that new?"

Her eyes darted down as her hand laid over the necklace. "Yeah."

"It looks nice." He took the moment to sweep her frame again, allowing his hand to gravitate to her waist. The fabric was smooth and slippery under his fingertips. "Actually, all of this is nice."

This nervous "Really?" slipped between her lips before she raised her head.

He scoffed. "You must know you look incredible."

A flash of uncertainty skirted across her face and his chest warmed.

Clark slid his hand from her waist down her forearm and brought her knuckles to his mouth. "Sadie, you are always beautiful, but you're distractingly breathtaking tonight."

A flush pinked her cheeks, and he had to keep his lips from curling up. She'd mastered the ability of controlling her blush with one exception—when she was falling apart beneath him. A sagging exhale left his body as he realized that because of his rules, he wasn't going to be able to see *that* flush tonight.

"Thank you," she murmured.

Giving himself an internal shake, he signaled the bartender. "Let me close my tab, and we'll get our table. You must be hungry."

Once everything was settled, he gestured toward the hostess stand. "Ladies first."

As his wife walked in front of him, he let his eyes drop right to where he wanted them.

·CHAPTER 13·

This grating sensation kept twitching between Sadie's exposed collarbones. As her husband pulled the chair out for her, understanding dawned. A similar sensation had plagued her the first time she'd undertaken an unfamiliar surgery. She was *anxious* sitting across the table from the man she'd been sharing a life with for four years.

Soft jazz music lingered in the periphery and the lighting and the decor of the glamorous restaurant was nothing short of perfectly executed, but at that moment, she would have traded it all for a messy code in the OR. At least in the hospital, she'd be able to get her footing. *And* she wouldn't be wearing this skin-tight contraption Parker had persuaded her to buy online the last time they'd been on call together. Since the dress was the only item she'd thrown in her duffle bag this morning, it was the only appropriate thing to wear to dinner tonight.

"I don't think we are going to be able to make the movie after this. Are you okay with just taking our time with dinner?"

"Yeah, that's fine." She unfolded her cloth napkin and draped it over her lap, somehow feeling better with its subtle weight over her thighs. "What were we going to see anyway?"

"The new *Wonder Woman* movie, but it just released, so we can catch it next date night." His voice held a hopefulness that twisted Sadie's stomach.

As she often did when nervousness bounced around in her body in front of Clark, she blurted out the first thing on her mind. "Wonder Woman is fine, but I've always been more of a Marvel girl."

A surprised chuckle preceded, "Really?"

Her shoulders bunched toward her ears. "Yeah. I just never said anything."

The soft look in her husband's eyes trapped her breath mid-inhale. "I'm glad I know now." Then a teasing smile twisted his lips. "I wonder what other secrets you've been hiding from me."

Sadie's mind raced, cataloguing all the places she *had* hidden from him, hidden from her daughter, hidden from her life. She'd picked up today's partial call shift to put herself in a place where she didn't feel completely out of control all the time. Shame bloomed hot in her stomach as her head dropped.

Clark's hand grabbing hers diverted her attention. "I like learning new things about you. That's the point of all of this."

The server greeted them, and after returning with a bottle of red wine, poured them each a glass. Sadie took a large sip, letting the bold flavors coat her tongue before swallowing, hoping the alcohol would soon soften the ache in her spine.

"What are you going to get?" Clark asked when they were alone again.

"Steak," she answered, having not even read the menu.

Clark's laugh sent warmth zipping to the tips of her toes clenched in her ballet flats. He shook his head, grin widening and eyes reading the print on the elegant paper between his fingers. "I shouldn't have asked."

After ordering and receiving their salad course, Clark asked about her day, and she felt her muscles loosening as she began detailing one of the more challenging cases she'd had that day. She'd needed extra hands tableside to hold the retractors to keep the muscle and fat out of the way so she could work.

Clark had his fork in his hand but hadn't taken a bite in several minutes.

Though that entertained gleam was in his eye, she had to ask, "Am I making you lose your appetite?"

He speared a layered section of grilled romaine. "Love, you've been telling me stories like this for years. If I had an issue with it, I'd have learned how to stomach it by this point." He brought the bite halfway to his mouth and then paused. "I actually like listening to you when you talk about work. You"—he shifted his shoulders as he searched for the word—"you kind of glow."

Her eyes darted to her own untouched spinach salad, gathering herself before glancing back up. Clark chewed with a satisfied look on his face. Her gaze snagged on Clark's tie—a shiny black one that matched the black collared shirt he had over grey slacks. The darkness of his attire, nearly matching his hair, only made the clear blue of his eyes more striking.

Before she could be distracted further by his raw attractiveness, she asked, "How was Lottie today?" Her brain racked to remember what day it was—Sunday. "You guys went to the market this morning?"

"She was good." He took a sip of his water. "And yeah, we were at the market this morning, but not just to walk around. I've been meaning to tell you about something new I've been doing."

"The project you've been working on?" She hadn't meant for the question to sound sad, but the emotion infiltrated her words.

He swallowed. "Yeah. Since the house is finished, I started some small woodworking projects. I've actually"—he rubbed his neck—"befriended a blacksmith." A chuckle escaped his lips. "I know that's a crazy sentence, but he sells his work at the farmer's market, and for the last four weeks, I've been selling the pieces I've made as well."

Her head tilted as her brows pinched. He'd been doing what? For a month? That guilty prickling sensation rose at the knowledge that she was not only missing her daughter's life but her husband's as she whittled away hours in surgery or hiding from her family.

Pushing down her discomfort, she asked, "What kind of pieces?"

"I can—" He dug his phone out of his front pocket and clicked through a few screens before handing it over to her. "I'll just show you."

On his camera roll was a picture of an incredibly intricate mosaic wood design laid within a slim rectangular frame for wall hanging. Her fingertips went to run over the wood and the image flipped to one of their daughter coloring on a wooden table set over asphalt.

"This one looks like the one in the playhouse." She lifted her gaze from her daughter's crayon-gripped fist.

"I was just playing around with the dimensions on the first one so I could build her one that would fit under the canopy tent."

She thumbed backward to see the decorative wood piece again. "Is this at home? Can I see it in person?" Something about the design made her fingers itch to trace each sharp angle. Her hand hovered over the screen before she gave into the impulse to touch and zoomed in on the image.

"I've got one like that and some other designs, though I've sold that exact piece." The smile on her husband's face could have fed her for a year. "Each one is a little different because of the grains of the wood and stain."

Her eyes caught and held his. "I want to see them all."

"Yeah?" His question was more of a breath.

Every time he'd completed a project in their home over the last few years, she'd always marveled at his work. It rivaled those seen on various home design shows. He'd always completed each carpentry project—and various other plumbing, electrical, and tiling ones—with such confidence and assuredness, it was odd that he was almost shy about this.

"Every single thing you work on is incredible. You've completely personalized our house, transforming it into something I couldn't have ever imagined. And with this . . ." Her eyes fell to the screen. "The way you visualize and then create these things with your hands . . . it's—" She exhaled. "It's beautiful."

He held very still before blinking twice. "Thank you."

Her lips lifted before her gaze gravitated to the glowing phone screen and an unexpected sourness tinged the back of her throat. Clark staying at home with Lottie meant that he wasn't completing large-scale projects for other people anymore. Something she knew he loved.

"Is this enough for you?" Her voice was low. "We can always put Lottie in day care if you'd rather go back to work full-time." She pushed the phone back over the table.

"This is what I want to be doing right now. I'm really enjoying it. If that changes in the future, we can talk about it, but you don't need to worry." His affectionate gaze made her pulse knock against her chin. "I'm right where I want to be."

◊◊◊

A comfortable warmth resonated in Sadie's muscles as she followed the taillights of her husband's truck home. She wasn't sure how long it had been since they'd been able to speak to each other without heavy pauses dropping between each sentence. Tonight, they'd simply chatted. And then as dinner had rolled on, they'd laughed and even flirted a little.

After parking in the garage, Clark took a few steps toward the main door to the house before she opened her car door.

"Wait."

He paused, pivoting in his black dress shoes.

"Your woodwork," she reminded him.

That unfamiliar bashful grin laced his lips again. "Right."

He flipped on the lights to the woodshop and brought her to a corner where more than a dozen pieces were stacked. "Those ones are finished."

Her greedy hands leafed through the sanded and sealed designs. Several prompted her to run her fingertips over the sharp, exact lines. She pushed aside one that looked like the center of a seashell before stopping at the visual representation of the feeling that surged through her body when her husband touched her—wooden lightning streaking through a wooden sky. She tilted her head. "These are amazing." Her gaze flicked up, and the pleased look on his face made her ache.

Clark cleared his throat. "We should pay Aurelia. She's probably wondering why we're home but haven't come inside."

Ten minutes later, they both eyed each other through the bathroom mirror, their mouths full of toothpaste foam. It'd been so long since they'd both gotten ready for bed at the same time. Clark's lips curled up around his brush. He spat and rinsed his mouth, stepping back and watching his hands in the mirror as he loosened the knot of his tie.

The whispered sound of him pulling the silky fabric from his collar woke her in a way that'd been dormant for months. Without thinking, she stepped in front of him, lifting her hands to slowly unbutton the black buttons over his throat.

"Sadie." Her name sounded as if it was being pulled over gravel. "We're not supposed—"

When her fingers pressed against the notch between his collarbones, his sentence halted in a sharp inhale. His lips parted as he watched her.

She let her gaze fall to the rapidly heaving fabric over his husband's firm chest. "We won't. I promise. I just—" When her fingers worked their way over his tightened abs, her own breathing became irregular. Her fabric-clenched hands were a half inch from his belt buckle. The sudden impulse to lick her way down the center line of his body was suffocating.

"Love." His hands covered hers. "I can't give you that tonight"—he paused until her dilated eyes found his—"but I can hold you." A pained expression flickered across his face. "I'd really like to hold you."

The truth escaped her mouth before her brain heard the words. "I'd like that too."

A small smile traced his lips as he turned toward their walk-in closet, tugging his shirt tails from his slacks. Sadie worked on scrubbing the makeup off her face, relieved that by the time she pulled the washcloth from her soapy eyes, Clark was already tucked under the covers. She took her time flossing her teeth and brushing out her hair, trying to calm the itchiness streaking down her arms.

After changing, she gave herself a shake and marched to the bed. When she flicked off her light and turned, Clark's expectant eyes made her stomach squeeze. She clumsily crawled over the gap between their sides of the king bed. It'd been so long since she'd lain this close to him, but when his muscled arm wrapped around her and nestled her in the crook of his shoulder, it was as if all the tension she'd been holding melted into his heat.

She became pliable as her breath evened out and the exhaustion of a call day plus a late night with wine finally tallied up. They didn't speak or say goodnight. Clark simply stretched his other arm to flick off his sconce before wrapping it around her. Her eyes adjusted to the darkness as she found herself memorizing the feeling of his steady frame beneath her, beside her—simply supporting her. Eventually, her eyelashes fluttered closed, and his slow, steady heartbeat was the music she listened to as she fell asleep in her husband's arms.

·CHAPTER 14·

Clark woke in the morning covered in a sheen of sweat and his wife's limbs. Her leg was pulled up over his abdomen and her hand dangled off the bed as her arm rested across his chest. Sadie's hair was matted around her face, her head still tucked into the nook he'd placed her in last night. His shoulder strained from holding her weight all night, but he couldn't have cared in the least.

When he'd asked to hold her, he'd expected her to lay in his arms for a few minutes and then shift back to her side of the bed. But when her breaths evened out and her limbs started to twitch as she crossed into sleep, he found himself unable to let go. It had been almost a year since she'd let him hold her like that.

Highly compressed elation pushed against the warm, heavy arm draped over his heart, and he shifted to kiss her forehead.

Only movement was a mistake.

The minute he shifted, Sadie made her humming-grunting sound and rocked her hips into his side. Her eyes were still closed as she wiggled her fingers and pulled back the dangling hand until it snagged on his bare chest. When her palm flattened and began to explore, her lashes blinked open. Their gaze held for two heavy seconds before she looked down at herself, having the same realization he'd experienced only a moment before.

He'd expected her to bolt to her side or maybe chuckle and scoot away, saying she had to get ready for work, but instead she watched her fingertips trace the ridge under his pecs. Clark bit back a moan as his eyes rolled closed with a halting exhale.

You idiot.

He knew he could resist procreation-minded Sadie, who only wanted one distinct part of his body, but he'd never been able to say no to this version of his wife. Not when he'd always wanted her as much as she wanted him. It had taken a truckload of effort to stop her last night, and that was before they were both half naked and in each other's arms.

When her thumb grazed his nipple, a choked, hissing sound escaped him. "*Love.*"

"I know." Her morning voice was raspy as her unfocused eyes raised and caught on his mouth. "The rules." She pressed her weight into the palm over his chest to raise herself, her gaze never lifting over his lips. "Just . . . let me kiss you."

He couldn't make his mouth form a refusal, and she took his silence as permission, shifting until she straddled his stomach, bracing her hands on the pillow on either side of his head and lowering her lips to his. Her kiss was sweet at first, but it quickly transitioned into something desperate, demanding. A groan left his throat as her tongue played with his, and he knew deep in his bones he wasn't going to be able to stop her if she asked for more.

Whatever she wanted, he'd give it to her.

Her hands weaved through this hair as she turned his head to kiss the line of his jaw and down the cords of his neck. A shudder ran through him when she reached his collarbone and licked. He'd been trying to hold back, but with that action, his hands grasped and squeezed his favorite part of her.

Her gasp washed over his skin before the baby monitor on his nightstand illuminated. A bawling Lottie could be seen stumbling out of her toddler bed, getting caught in her blanket and falling before standing up and moving to the door. Next the slamming of small hands against wood added to her sobbing.

Sadie bolted up, pushing against his chest with both hands. "I'll get her." She swung to stand beside the bed, running an arm around her face to tame her wild hair.

"When you"—her gaze swept low on his body—"get settled, will you come take over? I have to shower for work."

He coughed into his fist. "Yeah, I'll be right there. Just give me a minute."

The sexy half-smile on her flushed face did not help to achieve what he'd just been tasked.

Twenty minutes later, he and Lottie were finishing breakfast when Sadie hurried into the kitchen wearing her slacks and his favorite lavender blouse. Normally, she wore starchy collared shirts to the office. A small ribbon of joy pulled through him, thinking maybe she'd chosen the blouse because she was feeling happier this morning. She seemed lighter as she moved toward their small espresso machine.

He rose from the table, crossing to her. "I already made your coffee." He pushed the warm travel mug with her morning Red Eye into her palms.

"Thanks." Her gaze flicked from the mug to his eyes.

Everything in him wanted to lean over, to press his lips lightly to hers. Like on a normal morning sending her off to work. How things had been for years. But he wasn't sure when they'd snap back to reality. When this dream he seemed to be living in since he'd choked on whiskey at the bar would end.

Her mouth firmed into a line and part of him cracked.

This was it. He steeled himself for whatever happened next.

Her eyes dropped and she moved away—slowly, almost as if she was distracted or was pulling against a force that was trying to keep her in his presence. Sadie showered Lottie with kisses, smiling at their daughter's giggles and avoiding her yogurt covered hands. His wife made it two steps toward the kitchen threshold before she turned back.

"Linus says there's this new restaurant in Raleigh called The Yard. Apparently, it's got a huge patio with a fenced-in grass area with lawn games and a little playground. When his kids get antsy, he lets them play while he and his wife eat. I know it's a drive, but I could meet you and Lottie for dinner after work if you want."

"*Yes*." It had been a challenge not to interrupt her with that answer already. "I mean, we'll happily meet you there." Sadie's colleague Linus usually had good family-friendly restaurant recommendations, having four kids himself.

A small smile curved her mouth. "Okay. You should probably call and reserve an outdoor table."

"Done."

Clark waited for the sound of the garage door closing before he fist-pumped the air repetitively.

Lottie giggled between sips of apple juice. "Silly Dada."

His eyes flipped to the kitchen clock. "Let's clean up and go potty, little love. We've got to make it to class."

◊◊◊

Sadie was late to dinner after getting caught up with a call with the nursing director, but Clark didn't care. When she showed up, her smiles toward him made up for it and then some. She held Lottie on her lap, allowing their daughter to make a mess of her dress pants as she ate her buttered noodles. Even though this discorded unease kept fluttering at the edges of his mind, Clark intentionally pushed it away and tried to be present in the moment.

When Lottie had eaten half her meal, Sadie walked her through the playground a few times before the six-year-old girl at the table next to theirs adopted their daughter.

His wife sat down, keeping her eyes on Lottie. "I guess we've been replaced."

A laugh rippled over him watching the little girl hold Lottie's hand as she climbed the stairs. "Looks that way."

Sadie's eyes were still trained on their daughter as she smiled. The din of the restaurant fell away as Clark got lost in the moment. The sticky, hazy air was just beginning to soften as the sun lowered in the sky. This kind of light always made Sadie look like she was some kind of ethereal creature instead of the hard-as-nails woman she was. A sigh passed over his lips before the loud ringing of his cell phone broke the spell.

When he dug it out of his front pocket, his wife caught his mom's photo on the screen before he silenced it.

"You can answer it."

He set the screen face down on the table. "That's okay."

"What if she needs something?"

Sadie didn't understand that his mother often called just to chat. He knew that when Sadie talked to her mother, often when driving home from work, Penelope generally wanted something from her.

Clark opened his mouth to say his mother didn't need anything, but then decided to tell the truth. "They'd actually like to visit. They haven't seen Lottie since Christmas." His parents usually visited four times a year, but he'd made excuses for them not to visit in early spring like they normally did. "Maybe they could come down this weekend for the Memorial Day holiday? Lottie can show them her swimming skills at the pool. It should be hot enough for us all to swim."

They'd only been on good terms for less than twenty-four hours, but the desire to be back to normal scratched like thirst at his throat.

The skin around Sadie's eyes pinched before her lips parted to speak, and he tightened his abs for the blow. "I think . . ." She paused, glancing at Lottie again. "Okay." Her head bobbed. "That could be nice."

He barely kept *Really?* inside his mouth. "I'll call her on the drive home and let them know."

As dinner wound down, Sadie chatted with him about some resident drama, and he shared more details about his new business. Everything in him felt like it was loosening, like shaking his muscles out before a workout. By the time he'd paid the check and gathered up a whining Lottie, he'd banished that worrisome shadow telling him to second-guess his reality. When Sadie automatically leaned over to kiss him goodbye before they separated in the parking lot, his lips pulled away with a smile on them.

At last, everything was as it should be.

·CHAPTER 15·

Sadie counted silently in her head to encourage patience as she waited for the unit assistant in the ER to find her Dr. Duran—the man who was supposed to have met her in the cafeteria ten minutes ago. When a stinging sensation rocketed over her backside, she jumped four inches. "Hiya, toots" accompanied the slap, preventing her from immediately having the offender's head on a surgical tray.

"Parker, that's not professional." She turned, shaking her head as a smile curved her lips.

"I know." Her friend beamed. "But it's fun. You here for a consult?" The fact that Parker's scrubs were already covered with a freshly donned yellow PPE gown meant she was likely waiting on an alpha-trauma to roll through the ambulance doors.

"No administrative stuff, but the ER director's disappeared."

Parker's eyes twinged and flowed over Sadie's set of scrubs.

"I added on a surgery this morning, but I'm supposed to be doing director duties today."

"Ahh." She nodded before a slightly wicked grin tugged on her lips. "*So* . . ." Parker leaned into the word. "How was date night?"

It'd been three days since her and Clark's date. Since he'd looked at her like she was the most beautiful thing he'd ever seen and then had held her in his arms like she was something precious. Every day since had seemed a little lighter, the tension that used to sit between them had felt looser. It'd been easier and easier not to turn off in a different direction once she left the hospital complex and spend the evening hours curled up in a ball. Yesterday, she'd even driven straight home, catching the end of an impromptu backyard cookout with several of the dads and kids from Clark's fitness class.

A slow smile spread across her face. "Good."

Parker rolled her eyes and crossed her arms, causing the trio of multicolor hummingbirds on her left wrist to peek out from beneath her shirt cuff. "Really? You're going to go all monosyllabic on me?"

"Fine. It was better than good. It felt like"—she shifted her shoulders—"us. The old us."

"That's great." Her face lit up before she playfully punched Sadie in the arm. "Now you and Clark can go on a double date with Ivan and me. I've been wanting to try out that new distillery downtown."

"You're still seeing Ivan?" Sadie tried to keep the surprise out of her voice.

The fact that Parker was still seeing the sexy financial advisor that had brazenly approached their table and left his card six weeks ago was noteworthy. Usually by the two-week mark,

Parker would tout that things had "gotten stale" and began looking for a new man.

Her friend shrugged. "I'm trying something new."

Sadie opened her mouth but was interrupted by two quick blasts of a siren, signaling that the ambulance was here.

"Gotta go," Parker said before striding toward the ambulance bay.

Eventually, Dr. Duran showed up, and after wrapping up her meeting, Sadie headed to the on-campus building where their outpatient office was. She had a permanent office there, even though early in her directorship, she had generally headed home to complete her administrative tasks remotely once her meetings were done.

But after her second miscarriage in January, she'd been using this small grey room more and more. Sadie entered her office and sat at the computer to type out the decisions she and Dr. Duran had made about "synergistic practices" between their two departments. An hour or so later, when everything had been catalogued and sent off, her eyes drifted to the picture of her, Clark, and Lottie on their daughter's first birthday.

Her fingertips touched the cool metal edge of the picture frame as she gazed into the happy faces of the past. A smile lifted the corner of her mouth as she brushed a thumb over the glass protecting Clark's grinning face. Setting the frame down, she glanced at her computer screen. There was no reason that she couldn't finish the rest of her tasks at home.

Sadie pushed to her feet, gathering up her belongings, when shooting pain stretched across her lower abdomen, doubling her over. An agonized groan escaped her lips before she could inch forward to tap her office door closed. Awareness dawned that she was starting her period. Each time after was uncomfortable, but the pain she was experiencing now was nearly as bad as her last miscarriage.

She was prone on the carpet-tiled floor before her mind had caught up with the action. Scratchy carpet fibers poked at her cheek as a somber breath echoed in the empty room. The agonizing cramping only reminded her that she was no longer filled with life, as she should have been.

Though this time it had been a punch to the abdomen, there were times when the sorrow would unexpectedly sneak up on her. She'd be mid-surgery, or driving, or brushing her teeth, and one thought would prick at her consciousness. It'd start at a finite point, like the tip of her shoulder, and then diffuse through her whole body like a drop of dye in a glass of water, insidiously spreading throughout all her tissues and organs until she had to fight to stay upright and breathe through it.

After the worst of the cramping had subsided and she'd collected herself, Sadie drove blindly until her car sat in the familiar parking lot. The entire time she picked out, held the flimsy, slightly dirty plastic container in her hands, and stood in line to pay, she tried to ignore the cracking sensation in her chest.

Sadie dragged in a ragged inhale, and the scents of wood and soil in the hardware store jockeyed for her attention. She felt like she had many times before—that she had to pick one. Wood or Soil. Clark or her coping mechanism. She couldn't have both, even though that was what her heart yearned for.

As the older woman in front of her paid with a check, Sadie warred with herself internally.

This is crazy. You know that. You're a doctor. You have to acknowledge by this point that this is a compulsion. You need to talk to someone. You need to tell someone how you're feeling. You can't keep burying your emotions.

She shook her head.

It's fine. This is fine.

Silence was her companion as she finished the drive to the park on the other side of Northwood. Two weeks after that first flower had been planted, Sadie had found herself pot in hand at another well-manicured green space. Over the last year, she'd found solace over and over again as her locations had expanded from one to nine.

Eventually, she'd become more selective. The park couldn't be too small, unless there was a natural tree line because the plants would be discovered too easily. As kind as Deborah had been at Peaceably Park, she doubted she'd receive the same sympathy from other groundskeepers.

Sadie's tires crunched on the gravel of the eight-car parking lot, and a relieved breath left her lips finding it empty. Lake Trail Park was more of a large nature preserve than a park. There was a mile-long mulch trail around the man-made lake, one single ramada with a cement table, and a bathroom.

She dug her trowel out from the hidden storage bin in the back hatch and walked toward the side of the lake, mindful of the poison ivy that was flourishing everywhere. Minutes later, when she pressed the soil firmly over the third plant, she waited for that flooding sensation to pour through her veins. For the glimmering of relief to descend upon her after adding life to the earth because her body couldn't.

Only this time, it didn't.

This time, the shredding feeling in her chest matched the one that was ripping through her belly.

She stayed in a kneeling position for a long time, her forehead almost touching her forearms stacked on her quads. Eventually, she rocked back on her heels, pushing to an unstable standing position. Nothing was lighter. Only heaviness remained, pulling on her weary muscles, trying to disintegrate her bones.

Sadie gave herself over to gravity, allowing it to mold her with rough hands until she was rolled into her ball, perched on the nearby log. The sun began to dip behind the trees just beyond the water when her phone rang in her chest scrub pocket. She released the pressure of her thighs against her stomach enough to glance at the screen.

Clark's smiling face stared at her. Over the last few months, he'd stopped calling to ask if she'd be home for dinner. Generally, he'd wanted to know if he should go through the trouble of cooking a full meal, or if he could just eat a quesadilla with Lottie and call it a night.

Sadie knew he'd stopped calling because she'd so rarely made it to dinner. Somehow, after being home the last few nights, she'd apparently reset their behaviors. The screen glowed and vibrated in her hands before the call was sent to voicemail. She pressed it to her forehead with a halting exhale.

I'm sorry.

Sadie couldn't even say those two words out loud to the emptiness of the lonesome park surrounding her. They stayed trapped in her mind with all the other words she wanted to tell her husband.

Please help me.

I'm in so much pain.

If she let everything that brewed inside her out, she'd break open at the seam. A line would split down the middle of her body that even the talented Parker couldn't suture back together.

Parts of her weren't even *her* anymore.

Each time she miscarried, a percentage of her turned over to grief. Her body became marred and tangled. She wasn't even sure what segments were still her. A couple of ribs? Her ulna? The cartilage composing her nose?

How could Clark love this version of her? The version of her that was more broken than not. He'd only ever known her as a confident, accomplished woman.

He can't. The truth whispered on the breeze blowing across her face.

She wasn't the Sadie he'd fallen in love with. The woman who knew her place in the world because she'd fought tooth and nail to get there. The woman who commanded the respect of others.

Sadie looked at her trembling hands. This was the Sadie who struggled to put one foot in front of another and couldn't give him the family he wanted. That feeling of being a waxed version of herself, brittle and capable of crumbling at any point, rolled over her. Setting the phone on the decomposing wood next to her, she curled back into a ball—pressing herself back together.

You need to stay away from them. The best thing for them is for you not to be there.

Her phone buzzed with a text.

Clark: *Hey, love. I'm making spaghetti and grilled veggies. I'll make you a plate to reheat when you get home. Love you. See you soon.*

The mewling, splintered sound bursting from her lips immediately made her grateful for her solitude. Clark was expecting this morning's Sadie to walk through the door any minute now. The one who'd gripped his waist and pressed a kiss to his lips before leaving. Several desperate breaths seesawed through her tight lungs before her brain resounded with an answer.

You can't keep doing this to him.

Sadie knew she was causing Clark pain by not talking to him, by not letting the truth bleed from her veins, by shutting down and literally hiding, but she couldn't find another way to exist right now.

Her forehead thunked on her kneecap. She didn't want to let go of Clark, let go of Lottie, let go of their life together, but maybe that was the responsible thing to do. The *right* thing.

The stars dotted the sky, and she'd received Clark's "I'm heading to bed" text before Sadie allowed herself to finally drive home.

·CHAPTER 16·

"Is this, uh, the dad's exercise class?" A man in his late-twenties with thick, curly blond hair and glasses pushed a stroller toward the group just as Clark and several other dads were returning from their warm-up run.

"That's us." Miles smiled, gesturing to the circle of strollers. "Park your kiddo over there and pick a station."

"Oh. Okay." The dad stopped his stroller right next to Lottie's and pulled back the swaddle blanket that had been covering the attached infant car seat.

Most dads were doing a quick check of their kids before picking a station, but Clark simply marched to the one farthest away at the edge of the large ramada.

Acid had been eating at his intestines all morning, and now it was slowly working its way outward. Last night as he had waited for Sadie to text or call him back, he'd given his wife the benefit of the doubt. It had taken all of his mental energy, but he'd done it. After all, there had been times while things had been good in their relationship where she'd been out of reach while at the hospital. Even with constantly reassuring himself that everything was fine, he hadn't been able to rest after he'd put himself to bed. Only when he'd heard the whisper of the garage opening through the pitch black of their bedroom had he passed into sleep.

But then Sadie's leg hadn't been flung over the covers this morning like he'd expected. Light had pierced through the haphazardly drawn blackout curtains, illuminating the fact that he'd been the sole occupant of their large bed. As his bare feet had padded down the wooden stairs, he'd fought the itching sensation crawling up his back. His hand had rested on the garage door handle for several breaths before he'd confirmed what, in his heart, he'd already known.

Sadie was gone.

The dull ache that had settled just behind his breastbone felt like an old friend who'd come to grab a beer and catch up. Because in that moment, he couldn't lie to himself anymore. He'd seen this coming. He'd been holding his breath for days, waiting for the other shoe to drop. Even though a fool-hearted part of him had thought the progress they'd made in those short days was enough, he could no longer deny that maybe her motivations for staying away from him stemmed from something else. Something he hadn't allowed himself to think too hard about until now.

"Hey," Jayce jogged over. "You okay?" The rest of the dads were filtering to the different stations, but no one else followed Jayce to theirs.

Clark barely managed to keep his tone even. "Yeah, why?"

His friend took a deep breath and pressed his lips together. "No reason."

Miles had created a sports theme for this week's classes, and today's workout was inspired by football drills. An orange cone on the ground pinned down an index card with the exercise written on it.

Jayce bent to read it. "Five second mountain climbers into a sprint to the basketball courts, and repeat."

"All right." Clark braced his hands on the ground, waiting for the start whistle. The large cement slab, steady and unyielding under his palms, helped subdue the untethered feeling trying to capsize him.

"Clark!" Miles shouted from the circle of strollers. "Lottie says she needs to potty."

He barely stifled the curse wanting to stealth out of his lips. Right now, he *needed* to exert himself. He needed to push his body to its limits to prove to himself that he could control at least this—his bones, his muscles. Because everything else felt like it was outside his grasp.

When he swallowed hard and rose to standing, Clark ignored the way Jayce's eyes seemed to track his every move.

The entire time he re-Velcroed Lottie's purple sandals, unbuckled and picked up his daughter, Clark kept his eyes from the newcomer's stroller.

But it didn't matter.

The soft, grunting sound of the newborn fidgeting reached his ears regardless. Grief sucker punched him in the ribs, layering itself on top of all the uncertainty already plaguing him. Instantaneously, a sheen of liquid filmed over his eyes. He covered his shuddering inhale with a cough, even though only small children were around to witness its sound.

The situation didn't necessitate him sprinting with his daughter on his hip to the park bathrooms fifty yards away, but he did so anyway. Anyone watching would assume he was trying to keep his little girl from having an accident, not that he was running away from something that was inescapable.

Lottie giggling as they raced to the cinderblock building slightly assuaged the darkening storm brewing beneath his breastbone. After she went potty, he let her dawdle in the bathroom. She squealed as she stood under the high-pressure hand dryer, its forced-air pounding at her. Clark bobbed his head under the other one, letting his locks be flattened against his forehead. Her shriek of joy at the sight of him brought a genuine smile to his lips.

When they walked hand in hand back to the ramada, Clark almost felt he could handle the rest of the class. Except when he got back to the strollers, the newborn was crying—*hard.*

Miles called to him again, this time from his position kneeling next to Victor at the squat jump station. Victor was wincing as he removed his shoe as if he'd rolled his ankle. "Hey. Can you pick the little guy up for me? His dad ran to his car to get a bottle."

It wasn't uncommon for the dads to help with each other's kids. There was definitely a tribe mentality at Dad Bod Fitness, and Clark had helped out many times before.

"S—sure." The shaky word left his mouth as Lottie rose on tiptoe, pulling at the side of the stroller and peering over the edge of the infant car seat.

"Baby sad." Her tiny lips pulled down in a sympathetic pout.

He couldn't muster a response. Clark's fingers were clumsily unbuckling the red-faced and screaming newborn when Jayce screeched to a halt beside him.

"I've got him," his friend managed through heaving breaths, picking up the baby and quickly walking him to his father.

Though Jayce had just intercepted an infant—the most helpless version of a human being—it was as if his friend had just carried away a live grenade.

Clark blinked and rotated, surveying his surroundings.

Everything was proceeding as normal. The other fathers were completing different exercises at various points under and beyond the ramada. The children surrounding him babbled and munched on snacks, the sounds of "The Wheels on the Bus" softly playing from Miles's music player. The flowering scents of spring tickled his nose and the warm air wafted against his skin, but every inhale brought the sensation of nails tumbling down his throat.

Numbly, he buckled Lottie into her stroller, handed her a packet of goldfish crackers, and went back to class. Jayce eventually rejoined him, and Clark could tell that his friend was barely keeping the words he wanted to say behind his teeth.

Clark waited for physical exertion to alleviate the agonizing undercurrent of emotions streaking through his veins, but relief never came. Every second of class was a struggle. His muscles seemed to revolt at every command his brain threw at them. His head throbbed as if someone was repetitively striking it with a sledge hammer. When Miles blew the final whistle to signal the end of class, Clark collapsed back on his mat after his last sit-up.

Wispy clouds passed over the cheerful blue sky just beyond the ramada as a tiny pebble pressed into his back. Someone had put a wind chime high in the branches of a nearby southern live oak, and its metallic notes clanged irregularly as the breeze jostled it.

"Want to talk about it?" Jayce sat cross-legged on his mat.

About a week after Clark had confided to his friend about Sadie's miscarriages, he'd met Jayce at a kids' themed indoor play area/coffee shop after naptime. As their girls had enjoyed the gratuitous amounts of dress-up clothes, music toys, and fully stocked play kitchen, Clark had opened up about how challenging this year had been for him.

As a husband and father, *he* was the one who was supposed to protect and care for everyone else. He'd strived to be a pillar of stability for Sadie, for his daughter, while guilt over his own sorrow stabbed at his stomach. Because in the end, he'd only been emotionally impacted by each miscarriage—not physically like Sadie had been.

Jayce had listened and then admitted to having felt the exact same way. Clark had sat on a too-small chair, balancing a cold cup of coffee on his knee, but it had been like he could finally breathe after being held underwater.

"It's just hard today." He pushed up on an elbow, meeting his friend's eyes.

Jayce nodded. "I get it. Some days you can handle everything, and others just suck. Do you want me to take Lottie for a few hours so you can get a break?"

Clark sat and ran his hand through his sweaty hair. "Thanks, but my parents should be getting into town any minute. I need to head home."

"Okay." Jayce began rolling his mat. When they were both standing, his friend hesitated. "So, don't be weird about this, but I'm going to hug you, okay?" Jayce's eyes looked everywhere but at him.

His friend's discomfort made an unexpected laugh burst from Clark's mouth. He didn't have any issue with embracing another man but understood that some did. When Jayce's lips dove into a deep frown, Clark laughed even harder. Even though he tried to subdue his merriment, he couldn't stop from heaving with it until his abs ached.

"You don't have to be such an ass." Jayce wrapped his arms around Clark, heartily thumping his back for good measure, before pulling away with a shake of his head.

Clark stopped his friend's step towards the strollers with a hand to the shoulder. "Thank you." He met Jayce's gaze. "Seriously. That helped."

His friend's nose gave a quick upward nod. "Damn straight, it did. I'm an excellent hugger."

Clark couldn't help the wry twist tugging on his lips. "You sure are."

◊◊◊

His father's beat-up yet reliable Volvo was parked at the top of the driveway when Clark pulled into the garage. A second after he hopped down from his truck bed, his mom wrapped him in a bone crushing hug. Any other mother probably would have waited until their adult son wasn't sweaty and covered in grass, but Pam Benson had never been fussy about things like that.

"Hey, Mom." The familiar eucalyptus scent of her lotion was comforting as it simultaneously caused his throat to tighten.

"Gigi! Gigi!" Lottie bounced with excitement in her car seat until his father opened the rear cab door to free her. "Papa!" Her little arms gripped her grandfather's neck when he leaned down to kiss her.

"Hey, ladybug. I missed you too." His muffled voice held a smile, his face pressed into the car seat.

When his mom finally released him, Clark was prepared with the usual post-travel chitchat. How was the drive? Did you have much traffic? But then her intuitive hazel eyes snagged on his, silently reading him. A soldering iron poked in between his ribs. He should have known his observant mother would notice how unhappy he'd been.

His mom's face twisted with gentle concern as she laid both of her hands on his cheeks, just like she used to when he was a boy. "Oh, honey." She let out a long even breath. "What can you do about it?"

It was a phrase that she'd often used when he was growing up. Not in a dismissive way, like one would assume with an accompanying shoulder shrug or roll of the eye. The question was meant to jostle the brain into recognizing what was within your locus of control and what wasn't.

A thought rushed to the front of his mind. "Do you mind watching Lottie for a little while?"

·CHAPTER 17·

"This is Dr. Carmichael. I was paged," Sadie said in response to the greeting of the OR desk assistant's voice through her cell phone.

"Doctor, your husband's here looking for you. Would you like me to ask him to wait in the surgical waiting room?"

Sadie's next step down the ICU hallway faltered. Clark had never visited her at the hospital before. An icy sensation pulsed down her arms.

"Is Lottie okay?"

The assistant relayed the message, and in the background she heard her husband's quick denial followed by his breathy laugh as he explained something about surprising her with lunch.

A sagging exhale left her as she continued to the main hallway and began descending the stairs. Her daughter was okay. The momentary reprieve brought by that thought was instantaneously replaced by trepidation at Clark's presence here, at the hospital.

She forced herself to answer the assistant, "Tell him I'll meet him in the main lobby."

"Yes, Dr. Carmichael," sounded before she disconnected the call.

Sadie's gaze was unfocused while her long strides cut through the lobby.

"Hey, love."

As she spun, she had to control the funhouse mirror feeling that was squeezing all her extremities. Clark looked so out of place here amid all the scrub-clad workers and patients being pushed in wheelchairs with IV bags hanging aloft. The fabric of an unfamiliar white polo strained across his chest as one of his hands tucked into the pocket of his nicest jeans. For half a second, she got lost in the veins streaking down his arm before she collected herself enough to respond.

"Hi." Since her answer was more of a breathy exhale than a word, she swallowed and tried again. "I'm surprised to see you. Where's Lottie?"

A fragment of the light in his eyes dimmed.

"My parents arrived this morning, remember?"

An additional weight pushed down Sadie's spine. That's right. Now in addition to hiding her desolation at work, she'd have to play happy family for the weekend while Mike and Pam were visiting.

"Lottie was happy with them," Clark continued, "so I thought I'd come have lunch with you." His smile dropped even farther. "I called Maggie, and she said you had a gap between surgeries right now. I figured you would need to eat." His other hand raised the yellow striped bag from their favorite sandwich shop.

Chilled saline felt like it was being pumped through her bloodstream at the thought of Clark calling Maggie. The efficient woman managed the orthopedic surgery department's day-to-day schedule. At any point, Clark could call and find out that she wasn't in the OR as often as she claimed she was.

Though her body continued to war against her husband's presence here, her mind finally organized itself enough to answer. "That sounds nice. Let's eat in the courtyard."

Clark's grin found its footing again and before her chest could squeeze further, she turned and led him down the hall that opened to the large outdoor green space. Weaving through the stone pathways, past the sweeping willows, she found an unoccupied metal picnic table in the center of the courtyard. The space was crowded with other medical staff eating their lunches at the collection of tables, and patients and family members sat on the many benches tucked between hydrangea bushes and patches of yellow Carolina lupines.

She focused on even breaths as she unwrapped the waxed paper surrounding her sandwich. "Did your parents make it in okay?"

Her husband's laugh softened the nervousness singeing her skin. "You know my dad. He's got to be on the road by five a.m. to beat traffic. Plus, they were excited to play with Lottie." His tone became solemn. "They're looking forward to seeing you too."

She swallowed against the obstruction in her throat. "I might be late tonight. I'm booked through this afternoon." His lip began to downturn. "But I only have two-thirds of a day of office appointments tomorrow. Maybe we can grill something and eat dinner together on the deck."

Clark's gaze was unnervingly steady on her. "They'd like that."

Though birdsong, buzzing insects, and the conversation and laughter of many others surrounded their circular table, it felt as if they were encapsulated in stagnant ice compared to the vibrant life surrounding them.

"Is your sandwich good?"

"Mmm." She mumbled an affirmative sound over the large bite she'd just taken, nodding and blocking the view of her mouth. "Yours?"

Clark's eyes were on the uneaten sandwich held between his calloused fingers. Instead of answering her question or taking a bite, he set it down so slowly that a shiver raced down her vertebrae, stinging the base of her spine.

"What'd I do wrong, Sadie?"

"What do you mean?"

Her husband pinched the bridge of his nose with a loud exhale. "I'm trying. I'm trying to reconnect with you, with the dates and"—his hand swept over their discarded sandwiches—"and things like this, but you keep disappearing on me. Even now, you're looking at me like the sight of me makes you sick."

She cringed because it did, but only because she was reminded of how much she was disappointing him.

A tautness pulled at her right temple. If someone had told her that at thirty-eight she'd be the head of orthopedic surgery with a ridiculously attractive husband and an adorable daughter, she would've conducted a mini-mental exam to evaluate their connection with reality. But now that this was her life, she wanted to complete the vision that Clark had always detailed so realistically to her. A future she'd have never dreamed for herself—a happy little family of four.

That was why each time was so much harder than the last. That's why her brain couldn't reason away the overwhelming emotional pain as each life was ripped from her.

Sadie felt as if her lungs were paralyzed—air wouldn't leave or enter them. Stagnant carbon dioxide poisoned her from the inside.

"You don't make me sick," she finally managed.

"Then what is it?" His eyes bore into her, forcing her to focus on the shiny quality of the sandwich paper beneath her fingertips.

"You know what it is," she whispered.

His exhale pushed a few breadcrumbs closer to her. "Then let's talk about it. Let's work through it together." He paused. "Maybe we even need help. What do you think about seeing a therapist together?"

The muscles of her back pinched. The same thought had occurred to her only yesterday standing in line at Nash's Hardware Store, but having to talk to someone else made everything too real. If she told a therapist, if she told Clark, about what she'd done over the last year, they'd classify her as insane. Then she wouldn't be allowed in an OR, the only place that brought her any semblance of happiness right now.

"I don't—"

"Do you still love me?"

An aggregation of various nonverbal objections came out of her mouth, but no words. That question was ridiculous.

Across the table, Clark waited, the muscles in his jaw tightening.

"Of course I do."

"Because I haven't stopped loving you, not for a second, since that first night."

That statement hit her like a three-hundred-and-sixty-joule resuscitation pad to the chest, altering her consciousness. In the aftermath, stubborn intellect took its chance to grab the reins. "There's no way—"

His humorless laugh interrupted her. "Not every woman completely blows my mind in bed and then spends fifteen minutes explaining how she reassembled a splintered femur that day. I'd never met anyone like you. Of course I fell in love with you."

She could feel her cheeks reddening and fought hard against it. Everything that night had been in stark contrast to every previous romantic relationship in that she hadn't hidden any parts of herself. Before she'd always downplayed her assertiveness, her intelligence, and her love for her career.

That night, she'd gone full tilt, knowing that in the morning, she'd walk away and never see this handsome stranger again. Why bother making herself more digestible when it was just one night? The catch was that Clark hadn't seemed to mind. He'd only listened with this entertained spark in his eyes and insisted they see each other again.

Her husband frowned. "But I guess it wasn't the same for you."

Heaviness snaked through her chest remembering the rest of that evening. How after the hottest sex of her life and babbling about her surgical case, she'd accidentally fallen asleep in the nook of his strong shoulder. The loud pop of a three a.m. firecracker had brought her to consciousness first, but then his masculine, woodsy scent had snagged and held her attention. A few seconds later, he'd run his hand over her hair and down her spine in a way she'd never experienced before. When they'd made love for the second time, she'd struggled to mentally override the floating feeling beneath her sternum.

At her silence, her husband's face completely crumpled. "We wouldn't be together if it wasn't for Lottie, would we?"

Sadie watched in horror. It was as if all Clark's bones were being snapped in front of her, but she was powerless to stop it.

"Clark—"

He held up a hand, silencing her. "I just—" His voice pinched off as his tone climbed unnaturally high. His eyes darted around, seeming to remember that they were in a public place.

Clark stood abruptly, and she moved to do the same, but his face transformed. Hurt was replaced by this intensely fierce expression that stared her back down. The warmth of the metal seat seeping through her scrubs had previously been comfortable, but now it felt as if her skin was burning.

Then, for the second time in her life, she watched her husband's shoulders storm away from her. As hard as it was to see, the vision of him leaving solidified the fleeting thought that had reached out to her last night.

She needed to let him walk away.

She needed to finally put his needs over hers and let Clark go. He'd put her and Lottie first for so long. It would be the hardest thing she'd ever done, but hadn't her whole life been spent overcoming one hardship after another?

As soon as his parents left, she'd tell him it was over. Her chest squeezed, and she balled up her sandwich and threw it in the bag to give her hands something to do.

Once she'd cleaned the whole table, she strode toward the hospital.

Her fingers started to shake, and she consciously extended them before pulling her surgery schedule out of her white coat pocket. The thing she needed right now was cold OR air pressed against her skin and the whir of a bone drill. Not to focus on how after Clark's parents left, her life was over.

·CHAPTER 18·

Clark pulled a shirt over his slightly damp skin. Once he'd gotten Lottie down for a nap, he'd started helping his mom with her smart phone. But after over an hour, it had become obvious that it would take much longer than he anticipated to fix it, so he had excused himself to take a shower.

The sound of Sadie's laughter harmonizing with his mom's halted him at the top of the stairs—his hand gripping the banister for support. Though she'd said that she'd be home on time from her day at the office, she hadn't come home until everyone had been asleep last night and had left before they'd all awakened. If he hadn't gotten up with Lottie in the middle of the night, Clark wasn't sure he'd have even known she'd come home.

In the wake of Sadie's behavior over the past few days, it had become hard not to listen to that nagging whisper that'd been taunting him for months. After the first miscarriage, he'd assumed it was Sadie's grief that was forcing the divide between them. But maybe it wasn't.

Maybe she never wanted to be with you forever.

Though he'd fallen hard for his wife from the start, maybe if they'd never gotten pregnant, she'd have ended things a long time ago. Without Lottie, maybe this wouldn't have lasted.

As he descended the stairs, the back of his dad's half-bald head peeked through the large front glass windows. His father had his journal in hand, scribbling away. Even though a heaviness sat in his shoulders, a small smile reflexively curled on Clark's lips watching his dad work.

His parents had always believed you should do the thing you love. His father was a midlist thriller author but never seemed to mind that he never reached the ranks of Clancy or Baldacci. For him, the joy of creating each story was enough. The same was true of his mother who worked as a social worker for Adult Protective Services. She'd often said she couldn't have survived witnessing the things she did if she didn't love her job.

The philosophy in his house growing up had been that if you could support yourself with your chosen profession, you could do whatever you wanted. They'd never batted an eye when he didn't return to college and were always proud of him. They were actually embarrassingly complimentary of all the woodwork pieces he showed them and couldn't wait to sit at the market with him on Sunday.

The women's combined laughter increased in volume as he walked toward the kitchen. That hollowing feeling he'd been trying to chase away all morning punched him in the gut. This might be the last time his parents would visit like this. Sadie had said she loved him, but now he was second-guessing those words. She could have simply been placating him because he'd brought up the topic at the hospital, in public.

A deep sigh left him before he forced his feet through the threshold.

"But really, you need to tell me. How are women keeping their pubic hair these days? I always went full bush, but with age, the hair is thinning out down there. I think it's time for a new look."

A strangled, choking noise left his throat as he doubled back as quickly as he could, trying to retreat from his mother's words. In his haste to get away from the conversation he *definitely* did not want to hear, he ended up smacking his forehead hard on the sharp edge of the door jam.

"Clark." His wife shot from her seat.

"Honey, Sadie's home!" His mom beamed from her calmly reclined position at the kitchen table.

"Yeah, I see that," he said, his voice strained with pain.

Sadie's eyes narrowed as they focused on the part of his skull that was throbbing. "You're bleeding." She strode toward him, ripping off a section of paper towel on her way.

As starchy paper was pressed firmly to his forehead, he couldn't help the whimper that left his lips. The pressure of his wife's fingers decreased a fraction.

"Sorry," she whispered, her eyes momentarily darting and getting stuck on his. Time held for one . . . two . . . three breaths before her focus moved to his wound, lifting away the towel for inspection.

How much of this care and affection was genuinely hers, and how much of it was for the sake of appearances, Clark didn't know.

A gutteral tsking sound left her lips. "You really got yourself. I'm going to have to Dermabond this. Come on. I have some under the sink in Lottie's bathroom."

He covered the paper towel with his own hand. "Be back in a minute, Mom."

"I'll be here," she sang.

He followed Sadie's determined frame upstairs and waited as she released the child safety lock on the cabinet under the sink. His wife had brought home some hospital-grade products like the liquid sutures she was now looking for in case Lottie hurt herself.

"There it is." She set the pencil-shaped cylinder filled with purple liquid on the counter and shoved everything else back under the cabinet.

Even watching her sloppily pushing things back made his heart twinge. Clark had never met a messier woman, but damned if it never bothered him. He wasn't necessarily a neat freak—tidy, but not too strict about it. He'd seen clothes strewn all over, dishes in the sink, and stacks of mail on the counter of her two-bedroom townhouse that very first night and hadn't cared. He still didn't care. It was all somehow . . . just Sadie. She had this essence that he loved everything about, except now he was going to have to unlearn that instinct.

A pained cough came out of him when he realized that when they divorced, he'd eventually have to see her with the man she'd rather be with—passing Lottie back and forth like a baton.

"Why don't you sit on the counter?"

Clark sat and reached for their daughter's yellow polka dotted washcloth to clean his forehead, mostly to give himself something to do besides trying to avoid eye contact. The silence between them felt palpable, like he could reach his hands out and catch the wispy threads of it. They could even hear his mother softly whistling a James Brown song from her place in the kitchen.

"I'll do it." Sadie plucked the cloth from his fingers and let the sink run for a long time, staring into it.

"What are you waiting for?"

Her features softened when her eyes lifted to his. "It'll hurt less if the water is warm."

His heartbeat thrummed in his throat. No one was watching now. Her actions could be those of a wife still in love with her husband.

Or of a conscientious doctor, his mind countered.

His hand fisted, but Sadie missed it because she was testing the water temperature. She stood between his open knees and delicately touched the washcloth to his skin. He swallowed roughly when her natural scent hit his nose. Because of her job, she never wore any perfume, but the chamomile scent of her shampoo, mixed with something undeniably Sadie, could be caught at very close proximity.

Her lips parted as she focused on drying the wound. A cracking noise broke through the weighted silence, and then she was holding his hair back with one hand and steadily applying the liquid sutures with the other.

"It just needs a minute to set." She stepped back to toss the applicator in the trash. "Then you should be fine."

"I'm not fine," he rasped.

He hadn't meant the words to leave his lips, but there they sat between them. He hadn't been fine in a long while. He wasn't *going* to be fine. He wanted his wife, and he wanted her to love him back. Not knowing if she did was ripping him to shreds.

Misinterpreting him, she moved forward and examined his forehead again. The feather light touch of her fingertips added to the layers of pain surging through the rest of his body. He pressed his eyelids together to stave off the worst of it.

"Clark?" Her voice was thick with concern.

A hard swallow allowed him to separate his lashes.

Her pale green irises darted between his, her fingers still delicate over his temple. Then she inched forward and pressed her mouth to his more gently than she'd ever done in their relationship. Her head rocked forward until the center of their brows met with a heavy exhale before she kissed him the same way again.

He couldn't stop his hand from reaching up and brushing a thumb over the edge of her jaw. As her mouth found his a third time, her body leaned against the counter, against the insides of his thighs. When her tongue darted out hesitantly, a raspy breath sucked between his teeth. Then he pushed into her more firmly but still kept the slow rhythm as his tongue met and danced with hers. Her hands gripped and held his shoulders, kneading at indistinct intervals, depending on what he was doing with his mouth.

"Sadie . . ." He wanted to ask what this meant, but part of him worried that words would only make this intimate moment they were sharing fall away.

Her shallow breaths passed through her parted lips, millimeters from his, as she waited for him to finish his sentence.

"Dada!" Lottie's voice came from behind her toddler safety-locked door adjacent to the bathroom. "I wake."

His wife blinked and then looked around as if she was lost. When Lottie started knocking on her door, Sadie took a step back.

He tried to keep the grimace from running across his face. If only he could have had five more minutes, ten more minutes, screw it—a lifetime of kissing Sadie like this.

"Dada!"

Her shoulders dropped with an exhale. "I'll get her."

Sadie was out the door and opening Lottie's before he could reach out to stop her. As frustration raced through his veins, he ran his hand over his face, painfully snagging it on his fresh wound. The hard whispered expletive leaving his mouth weighed heavy with double meaning.

·CHAPTER 19·

Walking through the large tent-covered parking lot beside the small strip of shops on Main Street wasn't a new experience. Sadie had done it with Clark and Lottie a handful of times before she'd started signing up for weekend call shifts. Walking through the Northwood Farmer's Market with Mike and Pam in tow, carrying supplies from Clark's truck parallel-parked several blocks away, was completely novel.

Because of the holiday weekend, the market was decorated with all sorts of red, white, and blue banners and flags. There was a light and jovial feeling in the humid air, even though the heat from the asphalt seemed to be scorching her feet straight through her flip flops. By the time they'd made it to Clark's spot the second time, they were all covered in a fine sheen of sweat.

She'd seen all his creations in the woodshop, but seeing them displayed under a navy canopy tent with a modest woodgrain banner that read "Clark Benson, Woodsmith" was a different sight entirely. Two narrow banquet tables formed an L-shape, the panels either stacked on top or propped against the legs. As usual, her fingers itched to touch every piece. A design of layered sea stars and what looked like a wooden river flowing down the middle of a topographic map had been added to his repertoire.

Mike settled the kids' table and chair he'd been carrying to the right of the L-shape, creating an uneven U, before Pam unpacked the colored pencils and coloring book from Clark's grey backpack-style diaper bag. Sadie engaged the brakes to the stroller and unbuckled their daughter. Though she wanted to pull Lottie onto her hip and keep her there for the rest of the morning, she let her daughter join her grandparents for a snack around the small play table.

"How do you do all of this when it's just you and Lottie? There's so much to carry." The question left her lips before Sadie reminded herself that she was supposed to be minimizing her interactions with Clark, pulling away from him. She'd already made it infinitely harder by kissing him in Lottie's bathroom two days ago.

His eyes were cautious as they flitted up to hers. "We take trips. Or Thatcher watches her sometimes at his tent. He's always here super early."

"The blacksmith."

Clark's smile warmed that she'd remembered. "Yeah. You'll meet him today. And Robin."

Sadie swallowed over the excess saliva in her throat, knowing that today would be the first and last time she'd see the people who were now important in her husband's life. She forced her shoulders back and down. It was good he had so many people to call friends, who supported him since soon she wouldn't be able to.

"Sounds great." She made herself pull her gaze away from Clark's breathtaking blue eyes and busied herself straightening the smaller twelve-by-twelve designs on the front table. She rearranged them so her favorite designs were in the center before reverently tracing the lines with her fingertips.

"They're so intricate, aren't they?" Pam's warm voice was right beside her. "I always knew he had an artistic side, but it took thirty-five years for him to finally tap into it." A laugh burst from her mother-in-law's lips. "I suppose I have you to thank for that."

"Me?" Her eyes darted to Pam's twinkling hazel ones before noticing that Clark, Mike, and Lottie were gone. They'd likely headed back to his truck for the last of the wood pieces, the cash box, and the small computer he used for credit card transactions.

"Of course. You bring out the best in him. Always have." His mother picked up a small wood piece and brought it to her nose for scrutiny. "Not that he didn't create incredible things while he was working or doing all those projects at your house, but it's nice to see him trying something different. Expanding. Changing. We all have to do that. We all have to push out of our little shells and try to walk around naked a bit before finding a bigger one. You help him not to get stuck because you're always pushing your own professional boundaries. You're a good influence."

Tension pricked at the edges of Sadie's vision as congestion swelled at the bridge of her nose. Pam's words were incredibly kind, but they were also completely false. She wasn't good for Clark. Not anymore.

"I'm not sure you get this often"—Pam settled her hands on Sadie's shoulders—"but I'm proud of you, and I know Clark is too."

Sadie was glad dark sunglasses covered her startled expression.

"You must be Sadie." A deep baritone voice excused her from having to respond to Pam's words.

Her mother-in-law released her shoulders so she could turn to shake hands with the burly gentleman behind her. "Yes. And you're Thatcher?"

His sculpted mustache rose, revealing perfect white teeth over his beard. "That's me. Nice to finally meet you."

Sadie's heart snagged on "finally" while Pam introduced herself and then Mike as the trio returned to Clark's table. She tried to stay engaged in the conversation going on around her, but all she could focus on was how happy Clark seemed here. Halfway through Clark explaining how he created a piece, a woman who looked like a late-twenties version of Pam arrived by their group. Numbness pulsed up Sadie's arm as she shook the bubbly stranger's hand.

Lottie rushed to Robin's long billowy skirt, hands raised to be picked up. When this other woman settled Lottie on her hip and her daughter's happy fingers started playing with the dangling gemstones around Robin's neck, Sadie's breath punched out of her. Robin purred a greeting into Lottie's hair, and her daughter giggled.

The display table hit her bare leg before Sadie realized she'd backed away from the group. Their voices were taken over by this persistent ringing in her ears. She could see their smiling mouths opening and closing, their lips making words, but heard none of it. Sweat pooled under her arms and a drop ran from her neck below the collar of her tank top. Robin said something, and the whole group burst into laughter.

Sadie felt as if she'd been hit in the chest by an IV pole.

Clark didn't need her. He was better off without her. The evidence was in his joyous, careless, *dimpled* smile. A smile that had been missing in their home for nearly a year. He'd made all these friends, built himself a business and a community without her, and around these people he was happy.

Without her, he was happy.

"Are you okay?"

Sadie spun and was confronted with another tradesperson wearing a wide-brimmed hat and a bee-print apron.

The woman surveyed her face with a worried expression. "You're beet red. Do you need some water?"

"Sadie?" Clark's concerned voice sounded far away as his hot fingers singed her, bracketing her bare upper arms.

At last, a noisy breath dragged into her empty and burning lungs. "I'm sorry" was her exhale before her knees dipped unwittingly.

"*Love*." Her pet name was a panicked gasp as Clark gathered her tight to his chest. A split second later, he swooped her up, carrying her to the back of the tent under the shade before lowering her onto a plastic folding chair.

The crowd of people seemed to expand exponentially. Someone pressed a cold water bottle into her shaking hands. Another person draped a dampened handkerchief around her neck. Pam was using a twelve-by-twelve art piece as a makeshift fan. All while Clark kneeled in front of her, his nervous hands flowing over her body: pulling her sunglasses away, moving down her cheek, tracing her arm until he gripped her wrist, seemingly to take her pulse.

She wanted to tell him not to bother. To tell him there was no reason to check for a heartbeat because she knew the organ had disintegrated in her chest.

But like all the words she should have shared with her husband, those, too, were trapped inside her mouth.

"Do you want to go home?" Clark's worried eyes were on hers again.

"*Yes.*" The truth burst out of her. She wanted to go home with Clark and Lottie and have things be like they used to be. She wanted her family again.

He swallowed hard, the muscles of his jaw tight. "I'll have my dad bring his car around, and I'll get you settled."

Sadie halted her reactive wince. Of course. Clark had to stay here. This was his job now. He couldn't leave just because she'd realized that everything between them was truly over.

The wearied muscles in her neck complied only enough for a single nod. "Okay," she whispered.

He seemed to register her hesitancy. "Or I could—"

"No," she forced the pained edge out of her voice by clearing her throat. "Mike can take me home, and I can walk to the car."

His gorgeous irises darted between hers before she tore her gaze away.

Pushing out of the chair, she took Mike's extended hand. "Stay, Clark. You belong here."

·CHAPTER 20·

Wednesday evening, after wishing his parents a safe drive home earlier that afternoon, Clark tried to turn his frustration into something positive. But after forty-five minutes of trying and failing to coerce angled slivers of wood into their design frame, he turned off the compressor. The release valve sent the hissing sound of shooting air into his workshop. An awkward laugh almost bubbled from his lips because a similar pressure had built up within himself over the last few days, but there was no release valve in sight.

He scrubbed his free hand over his face with a nasally exhale.

Things had been so much worse since Sadie had overheated at the farmer's market. Even his ball-of-sunshine mother had noticed the shift and exerted pallet-loads of energy trying to lift Sadie's spirits at every turn. His father, a known quiet introvert, had begun engaging Sadie in conversation whenever they shared a room. Often his wife would politely smile and nod along, but the moment his parents' attention was diverted, a deep frown would crease her lips. Even their daughter's presence hadn't had its usual brightening effect.

Maybe Clark should have come home with her Sunday, but for months it had been impossible to know what the right course of action was, so he'd listened to Sadie's words and stayed. If he'd taken her home, he might have gotten the version of his wife that had flickered back into life after their date, or he could have gotten the version that had refused to talk to him when he'd brought sandwiches to the hospital.

Clark almost felt seasick with the unpredictability of his life right now. It was as if the physics of gravity were constantly changing, and he was stumbling to get his footing.

And then there was the other part of him that was already mourning, already anticipating that things wouldn't get better from here.

Had he known that Friday afternoon would have been the last time he'd have heard his wife's careless laughter, he would have savored the sound. Had he known that he'd only get one chance in his life to have Sadie's gentle, tender kisses, he would've slammed the bathroom door shut and ignored the world. Had he known that the last time he would have held his wife to his chest was on that hot Sunday, he wouldn't have let her go.

Only . . . in the end, it wasn't an issue of him not letting go. It was that she kept pushing him away. There was only so much he could do before he had to resign himself to the fact that Sadie didn't want him.

The muscles in his shoulders tensed.

"You can't force someone to love you," he murmured.

Even though he kept making his brain tell him things like this, to prepare himself for their inevitable separation, his body fought like a fierce, stubborn toddler against the idea. A foolhardy part of him writhed and kicked internally, refusing to relent to the harsh reality before him.

Clark started tidying up his tools, putting them back in their designated places to distract himself from the deep sinking feeling vibrating through his muscles. He ignored the bile stirring at the back of his throat as he turned off the window AC unit and flicked off all the lights.

Stepping into the muggy evening air, the sound of a running engine and his mother-in-law's shrill voice could be heard over Sadie's car speaker. Seeing his wife's car tucked into the garage beside his truck used to bring a smile to his lips, but now deep creases tugged at his face.

Emptiness at the thought of his wife's crossover never occupying the space again was interrupted by Penelope's contemptuous words. "I'm sure Pastor Noel appreciates you calling him, even though he's a man of God, so he'd never say otherwise. I told him I wasn't sure you could even help since he's having heart issues and you're a *bone doctor*." The last two words were said with such disdain Clark's nose wrinkled reflexively.

His wife's voice was tight. "I just helped him get in contact with a good cardiologist. He only wanted a recommendation."

Though Clark hadn't spent a lot of time with Sadie's family—they never visited, even though they only lived three hours away in Florence, South Carolina—from his limited interactions with Penelope, he got the distinct impression that she was not happy that her daughter was a surgeon.

Which was mind-boggling.

Every day he was proud of his wife.

That gut punch sensation hit him again, knowing that soon she wouldn't be his to be proud of.

Clark focused on the group of fireflies weaving and dancing across the nearby patch of grass as his breathing evened out. He should grab the spare key from the playhouse and go into the house through the door to the deck. With things as strained as they were already, he didn't want Sadie to think he was eavesdropping on purpose. He took two long strides away before Penelope's harsh words halted his movement again.

"I guess that's helpful, but really, if you had to be a *doctor*, couldn't you have been a pediatrician or something? At least then, all your nieces and nephews could have had free care. Then you could have actually been of some use to the family."

Clark's fist clenched at his mother-in-law's words. What a toxic catch twenty-two. Penelope wasn't proud of her daughter but still expected her free medical council.

"I prefer to work with adults."

A forced laugh preceded, "I'm aware, shug. You're not great with kids."

Irritation vibrated across his shoulder blades as Clark spun to face the back of Sadie's pearl white crossover. His wife was a tender and attentive mother, and the handful of times he'd seen her with her many nieces and nephews, she'd been the same way with them. She'd been working more than usual lately, but the minute she was home, Lottie was in her arms.

This is a bunch of—

"It's a wonder you found yourself a man like Clark to take care of that daughter of yours because Lord knows you couldn't do it yourself. Not when you're always running off to the hospital. You know what your problem is, Sadie Love? You're selfish. Always have been, always will be."

"I know." Sadie's head bent until her forehead was resting on the steering wheel.

Clark unintentionally took a step back. He'd never felt that Sadie's time taking care of others was selfish, but did she? She was helping their community in a way few were capable of doing. Anybody can build a set of shelves or collect pieces of wood together in an appealing way, but few can reassemble bones and save lives.

"That on top of your"—she cleared her throat—"larger size and the fact that you simply can't be bothered to do something with your hair or put some color on. Honestly, I don't know how he puts up with you."

"Me neither." His wife's words were a defeated breath.

What the hell?

Sadie was agreeing with her mother? His incredibly strong, capable, intelligent wife with whom he was insanely in love with was agreeing with this vile woman who's only contribution to society had been painted nails and a smile.

How long had this been going on? The way Penelope talked to Sadie almost sounded like a script, like a well-worn tirade she repeated over and over. His heart squeezed thinking of how much abuse Sadie must have endured over the years, how it had happened right under his nose for years, and he hadn't known.

Instantaneously, his mind started sprinting in a different direction.

How much else had Sadie kept from him?

He'd always trusted Sadie, never doubted her when she said she was working extra shifts or had added on surgeries, but what if she hadn't been at the hospital all this time?

What if she'd been spending her time elsewhere? What if all these early mornings and late evenings weren't whittled away in the OR or on call? What if she was already spending time with the man she'd rather be with?

A cough burst from his lips, and he slapped his chest against the splintering pain below his breastbone.

"Any. Day. Now." Penelope's enunciation of each word brought Clark back to the driveway. "I said it on your wedding day, and I'm saying it again now. Any day now, that man's gonna wake up from whatever trance he's in and realize that he's too good for you."

Penelope had told her own daughter on her wedding day that she wasn't good enough *for him*? If anything, it was the way around.

Before he could revert back to the tail-spin he'd been in moments ago, his wife's sagging sigh and broken words penetrated his bones.

"I know, Mama. I don't deserve him."

Those weren't the words of a woman who was cheating on her husband. Those were the resigned words of an overworked woman whose husband hadn't protected her from her own malicious mother. Whose husband hadn't taken care of her when she'd been unwell on Sunday. Who was constantly assuming the worst of her.

Christ.

The dropping, hollowing feeling in his stomach morphed as adrenaline took over. At least he could fix this one thing right now. His boots slammed the concrete as he strode to the driver's side and flung the door open. Sadie's head popped up, her mouth gaping, and her eyes wide.

"Penelope, I need Sadie. She'll call you back." Then his fingertips punched the steering wheel disconnect button.

·CHAPTER 21·

"Does she always talk to you like that?" Her husband's voice was brimming with outrage.

Sadie tried to shrug, but with the weariness from the long day and then the onslaught from her mother, her shoulders barely raised a few millimeters. The air escaping her slumped body left with the force of survivors trying to vacate a sinking ship.

"Ever since I can remember."

Clark's left eye twitched, and his face twisted as if he'd swallowed a putrid lemon rind. "That's *bullshit*."

She sat back against the driver's seat, shrugging fully this time. "It's all I've ever known."

"That's wrong. She shouldn't speak to you—" He cut himself off. "Why'd you agree with her?"

She tensed, and then decided to lie. "It's often easier to simply say, 'yes ma'am,' than to argue."

Clark eyed her, and she felt herself growing warm under his scrutiny. "Tell me you don't believe her."

Her hesitation set off something in him. "Because she's *wrong*."

Unable to take the tight set of her husband's jaw, she lowered her gaze to the garage floor between them. Tonight, she was supposed to tell him that she was going to pack a bag and check into a hotel for a while, that it would be best for him if she wasn't around, but his indignation on her behalf was only making her chest hurt more than it already did.

"Love, look at me." His soft words drew her attention unconsciously. "You're an incredible surgeon. I *know* you know that. You're not being selfish by helping people in our community, by helping your colleagues. How many times have you spent extra time helping different residents perfect their surgeries so they could do the most good for the public?"

Her mouth moved, but no words came out.

A small, tender smile rose on her husband's face. "And you're an amazing mother to Lottie. I know you've been busy lately, but when you're home, you two are inseparable. You'd never speak to her like—" He cut himself off again, shaking his head.

Clark seemed lost for a moment, his gaze fixed on the messy clutter covering her passenger seat. In the absence of his attention, a swell of guilt sideswiped her. What would spending time with Lottie look like once she no longer lived here?

When he lifted his face, those striking blue eyes bore into her. "Why did you agree with her about me?"

Her stomach clenched painfully as exhaustion pulled at every fiber of her being. She didn't want to list all the ways that she wasn't what Clark should have. All the ways she was letting him down by not being "woman enough." Seeing him happy without her on Sunday had already been excruciating.

"It's her, isn't it?" That hard tone edged his words again. "She's taught you there's something wrong with the way you look." Clark swallowed, his gaze far off, even though it was trained on her face. He blinked back into focus. "There's nothing wrong with the way you look. Do you know how many times I've thought of another woman since I've met you?"

She subtly shook her head, not truly wanting to know the answer. Surely, the number had to be in the thousands.

"Not once."

Shock quaked through every cell in her body. *That can't be—*

"*Not once* since I kissed you that first night have I even thought of anyone but you. I mean, Jesus, Sadie"—he ran a frustrated hand over his hair—"you're perfect."

She couldn't help but to wince at his description of her.

"You are." His tone was insistent. "Look at you. Let's put aside the fact that your fingers literally put people back together on a daily basis." His hand gestured over her body and then his lingering gaze followed it, setting her aflame. "Your skin, your hair, those curves that fit perfectly in my hands"—his words hardened as his anger transformed into something else entirely—"and that incredible ass."

She couldn't formulate a response to his words, to the intensity at which they were shoved in her direction.

"Get out of the car." His hand clenched the door frame.

Her muscles took a few seconds to respond to his command, but once she did, he closed the door and backed her against it. Each palm flattened against the window on either side of her face, his legs bracketing her own. Alarm bells rang through her mind, reminding her that she was supposed to be pushing him away, that she was supposed to be leaving tonight, though her body simply softened beneath his.

She was powerless when he wanted her like this. She'd always been.

An intense wildness that she'd never seen before took over his features as he muttered something unintelligible, only catching "show you."

When he was a fraction of an inch from her lips, he paused and pulled back. "I'm sorry."

"For what?"

His lips dove into a deep frown. "For not knowing that your own mother treated you like that and protecting you from it. And for not telling you every day that you are my idea of perfection. You were always so self-assured in everything, I thought that meant with this too. I thought you knew." His mouth inched closer to hers as if drawn against his will. "I thought you knew what you did to me. How you drive me out of my goddamn mind." The last sentence was roughly growled over her lips.

Instead of devouring her, his close-lipped kisses teased and toyed with her until her own tongue darted out. The minute it touched his skin, he instantly morphed into the untamed version of her husband she was familiar with. But now every movement of his hands and body, framing and tilting her face so he could explore her mouth deeper, his chest pressed intently against hers, took on another meaning.

They'd always had a chemistry that was undeniable. When Clark's hot hands were on her, she'd forget her insecurities. She'd move into this alternate dimension where anything was possible, but she'd always doubt herself afterwards. That little voice that her mother had instilled in her since birth always whispered that she was wrong, that he couldn't possibly feel the same way about her that she did about him.

Those hot hands were now exploring her body, squeezing and pulling at the fabric of her scrub top. When the pale green cloth passed over her face, reality came back in a sharp gasp. She needed to push him away, she needed to leave. Her mind searched for something to say, anything, to try and do the right thing.

"Your rules."

His hoarse words zipped down her spine. "Screw the rules."

When he picked her up with one arm and compressed her against the car again, his mouth over the nook of her neck, Sadie gave in. She wanted this as much as he clearly did. She might be a *terrible, selfish* person, but she wasn't pushing her husband away tonight. She couldn't.

The window pressed the metal clasp of her bra into her skin until it stung. Then Clark pulled her forward and marched her up the four stairs into the house. Once inside, he took a sharp left into the downstairs guest room before tossing her on the bed.

This devilish smile crossed his face as he stood over her, chest rising and falling rapidly. His fingers tickled her ankles as he slowly tugged one clog off and then the other before reaching up to pluck loose the bow holding her scrub pants up. He drew her pants off with a pace that maddened her before leisurely reaching behind his head to pull off his T-shirt. Clark looked like a starved man, and she was a juicy red apple as he crawled over her.

"You have to understand," were the last words he said before he showed her again and again what he meant.

◊◊◊

The air from the AC pricked Sadie's naked skin as a slant of light pierced the room from the open window. She bolted straight up in bed, getting her bearings. The guest bed comforter clenched between her fingers as she noticed Clark's resplendent body to her side, facing her. Her head snapped to the mantle clock that sat on the grey dresser—6:45 a.m.

"Shit."

She jumped from the bed, nearly tripping over her discarded clogs. Her phone with her alarm that would have woken her up for her seven o'clock OR slot was still in the car with her messenger bag where she'd abandoned it last night.

Her movement startled Clark out of his slumber, and a lazy smile came to his face before he recognized her panic. "Are you late?"

"Yes," she hissed, trying to decide if she should pull on the dirty scrubs on from yesterday but was unable to find where he'd flung her underwear.

He stood quickly. "Run upstairs and get changed. I'll call Maggie and tell her you'll be a bit late."

Even in her rushed state, her gaze stalled a second on her husband's gloriously naked body before she darted up the stairs. When she returned a handful of minutes later, he held out a travel mug for her.

"I didn't have time to make espresso. Coffee will have to do today."

Her hand grasped it, and she was halfway pivoting to the garage door when the sensation of his fingers under hers traveled up her arm and registered in her brain. Suddenly the onslaught of all the emotions she'd felt last night flooded her system.

Maybe she really was enough for him—just like this.

Everything else happened in coffee-scented slow motion.

The metal mug made a clunking sound on the granite island. His puff of surprised breath when her chest hit his blew over her face like a gentle breeze. The heat of his boxer brief-clad body speared through the thin fabric of her scrubs as she pressed him against the counter.

Though she knew she'd surprised him, he wasted no time matching the hungry need of her lips and tongue with his, his hands gripping and tightening as firmly as hers did around his shoulders.

"I love you." Those were the only possible words that could have come out of her mouth when she broke the kiss.

His fingers bracketed her ponytail, bringing her lips back to his for a knee-weakening sweep before his forehead touched hers. "I love you so much. I don't think you have any idea."

Light flooded her chest as her lips rose in a smile. That cocky confidence that she'd had early in their relationship that they could beat the odds, that what they held between them could be enough, brightened within her.

"Now get." He grinned. "Go put people back together so you can come back home." He gave her backside a squeeze with his words, and for the first time in a long time, she wasn't looking forward to a long day of surgery.

·CHAPTER 22·

Sadie's calendar had her booked until four in the afternoon, but for the last two months that meant she usually came home around seven—just in time to tuck Lottie into bed and then disappear into the study to work on charts. So when Clark was lifting their daughter from her car seat after getting home from swim lessons at four-thirty and Sadie pulled into her slot beside him, he tried to prevent disbelief from displaying on his face.

"Hey." He set a wiggling Lottie on the ground so she could run over to his wife.

Sadie settled their still damp, swimsuit-clad daughter on her hip. "Hi." The smile she sent him stole his breath, and he had to tighten all of his muscles not to stumble backward. Fortunately, she switched her attention to Lottie. "Did you have fun at swim lessons?"

"I fish!" Lottie beamed.

"I bet you are. Do you want to show Mommy tomorrow? I got my call shift covered so I could have the day off. Maybe we could all go to the pool? As a family?" The last question brought her eyes up to his with an uncertain, questioning look.

Something dawned on him at that moment. With everyone else, in every other situation, Sadie was a confident kick-ass woman. Only moments like this, with him, had she ever shown her vulnerability. His heart pounded thickly in his chest with the knowledge that he was the only one she trusted enough to show this side of herself.

"I think that's a great idea." He tried to keep his words light, though emotion jelled his throat.

His wife's relieved, relaxed smile made his entire day—his lifetime.

He didn't think. He only responded. Two sure steps brought his lips to hers, his hand behind her head tilting her face in that perfect way so he could taste her more thoroughly. Only Lottie pounding her little hands on his shoulder brought him back to reality.

"Squish. Dada, I squish."

"Sorry, little love." He gave Lottie's chin a gentle pinch as he pulled back.

Sadie's dazed, unfocused eyes blinked at him before they turned to respond to Lottie's words.

"I do it too." Her little hands roughly grabbed Sadie's head before kissing her ear.

The musical sound of his wife's laughter as it wove over and under their vehicles, bounced off shelves and walls, warmed Clark in a way that he'd been worried was irreparable. Last night he hadn't only been able to hold his wife, he was pretty sure he'd convinced her that she was everything to him. Today, with her being here, with her laughter filling the air that entered his lungs, it was almost too much.

Slightly concerned his heart would explode in his chest, he moved to hang their wet towels on the clothesline strung beside his truck and put away the swim bag.

"Can I do her bath?" That uncertain tone was weaving its way through his wife's words again.

"Yay! Mama wash!" Lottie's hands were raised in the air before he could even respond.

He smiled larger than he had in months. "I think you've got to now."

The evening felt so much like a blissful mirage that he had to fight against the doubting suspicion that it wasn't real. At one point, he'd even crossed his arms to conceal himself pinching his bicep. It was like the last year of their lives had been peeled away. This was how it'd been before, Sadie attentive and playful with Lottie, affectionate with him. Home—the three of them together.

Even when her phone rang with the hospital's caller ID, she looked at him with an apologetic tilt of her head before she ducked away to answer it. Normally, she'd just bark "Carmichael" into the phone and disappear into the study.

Whatever fire she was putting out at the hospital took longer than he expected, so he put Lottie to bed by himself and was comfortable on the couch before Sadie reappeared.

"Sorry about that."

"It's okay." He paused the popular western drama he'd been watching. "Want to watch something together?"

"Sure."

He flipped to the on-demand list of movies. "You know, you were so close to being my perfect woman except for the one thing," he said, toggling to the Marvel Studios list with a smirk on his face.

Sadie was watching him instead of the screen, brows pinched.

"Which one's your favorite?" He gestured to the TV.

When her face returned to his, this hand-in-the-candy-jar smile crossed her lips, and he had to fight hard against the impulse to grab her waist and drag her onto him.

She sat close, but not right next to him. "*Iron Man*."

A button push started the movie, but only thirty seconds of "Back in Black" played before his wife was straddling his lap, her fingers weaving through his hair, lips on his.

◊◊◊

As Clark brushed his wife's hair back over her naked shoulder, a nervous anticipation threaded through him. He was going to purposefully fracture the glass. He was going to break the peaceful treatise they found themselves in, but he needed to know that this could last. He needed to know that they could communicate with more than their bodies.

At least he'd been smart enough to see that flush take over her skin first.

After they hadn't watched a single scene from *Iron Man* last Thursday, Clark had told himself he'd give it a week—a week before he broached the subject. After all, it had been a long hard year of slowly drifting apart, and now everything felt too blissful to try and burst it intentionally.

After the fun family day at the pool last Friday, he'd paid Aurelia double to come over at the last minute so he could take Sadie to a downtown summer music festival. They'd danced, drunk beers, and ate funnel cake, even though the June evening was almost too sticky for a hot snack. Then, after the sitter had gone home, he'd traced his tongue over every one of the subtle tan lines Sadie had developed at the pool.

Every day since then had been better than the last. Sadie had come home on time every night, given him a stirring kiss, and then taken Lottie on a new adventure—tromping through the woods behind their house, hunting for worms in the soil, playing pirates in the playhouse. His wife had ended up so filthy that she'd taken to showering with Lottie. Then they'd both be clean and in fresh pajamas for bedtime.

His chest had almost burst watching his two damp-haired beauties giggle over picture books. On those days, two seconds after the toddler lock had been secured on Lottie's door, he'd swooped Sadie up and carried her laughing body to their room. Later in the week, however, pervasive doubt kept creeping into his subconscious, making him wonder if he'd hit his head and was in some sort of fever dream.

So he'd let Sadie put Lottie to bed while he did the dishes or worked in the woodshop. But as soon as their daughter had fallen asleep, his wife found him. Then they'd end up a tangle of limbs on the kitchen floor, or he'd have to engage the brakes on the casters of his mobile worktable before lifting her atop it.

The entire time, he kept waiting for the other shoe to drop. For something to ruin this—something outside his power. Everything had been so up-and-down over the last few months, it was nearly impossible for him to get his bearings. Part of him foolishly hoped that since he'd shown her how much he loved her, how much he desired her, something had shaken loose in both of them. That something silent and powerful had transpired between their hearts even though no words except "I love you" had been exchanged.

But now he needed to know. There were lingering questions that had been buzzing through his mind all week that he needed answered. They needed to talk about what had happened between them over the last year. They needed to talk about their future. He needed to know that things wouldn't change with the snap of a finger and he'd be back to loving her from a distance while living in the same house.

"Love?"

"Hmm." Her auburn lashes fluttered open from her space next to him on his pillow.

Part of him wanted to keep the words trapped in his mouth and kiss her again.

No. He shook himself internally. *We need to sort this out.*

He let his hand run down her side and rest on the sweet curve of her hip. "I love you—"

"I love you too," she interrupted, pressing a kiss to his lips.

He bit back a groan at her taste lingering on his tongue. Maybe he should have done this fully clothed in the kitchen, or outside, or in a restaurant.

His fingers weaved through her hair. "I want to talk about us."

She stiffened slightly, as he'd known she would. "Okay."

"I've noticed that even during this last week when things have been so *incredibly* good, we still don't talk." He kept his gaze soft as it focused on her face.

"Sure we do."

"No," he said gently. "We don't. We make love to each other and we co-parent, but we still haven't talked about the fact that it feels like we stepped out of a one-year time warp. I'm"—he swallowed—"I'm afraid we're going to go back to not connecting, and I'm not sure I can take that again. I need us to try to get on the same page." His thumb framed her jaw. "Do you think we could do that? Can you do that for me?"

She seemed to be warring with herself as her irises darted between his, but in the end, a subtle nod shook their shared pillow.

"Really?"

"I don't want to lose you." Her words were barely a whisper.

"You could never lose me." Sadie's relieved exhale washed over his lips as he brought their foreheads together. "I'm right here. Whenever you want me, I'm always right here."

Then those soft kisses, like the ones they'd shared in Lottie's bathroom, rained over his mouth, and he lost the ability to breathe. Only when she climbed on top of him, pulling him back from the emotional abyss, did he gratefully regain control over his muscles.

·CHAPTER 23·

"Talk," Sadie muttered to her soap-sudded hands, scrubbing into her last surgery of the day.

Even the word by itself sent this itchy tension crawling up her spine and unease volleying between her shoulder blades. Late last night, they'd agreed that today, after Lottie's bedtime, they would sit down and have the conversation that she'd been avoiding since her first miscarriage.

Though she'd gotten this far in life without having to expand on her inner workings, she had the ominous feeling that that was about to change. Growing up, her brothers had bullied the small, flickering instinct to put words to the emotions that stirred in her veins.

Mad at Alden? Sucker punch him to the ribs and run. Don't bother trying to explain that him destroying the stethoscope Auntie Beth bought you for Christmas meant you'd lost your most prized possession. Sad after finding a dead baby bird? Don't let Duke see the tears in your eyes—he'll never let you live it down. Terrified of the dark? Don't let Jasper know that you hug an illuminated flashlight once everyone else is asleep.

The only emotion she understood growing up was love. Every time her father picked her up and placed her on his strong shoulders, affectionately called her "my girl," or defended her desire to play soccer instead of take ballet lessons, she felt this overwhelming warmth flood her muscles. Daddy had been the only person who'd truly understood her. Who'd loved her just as she was. Who'd never asked her to change.

Until she met Clark.

"Prepped and ready for you, Dr. Carmichael," Baylee, Sadie's favorite circulating nurse, called out from the swinging OR doors.

"Be right there."

Baylee's verbal nudge alerted her that she'd been scrubbing for too long. The reason Baylee was her favorite was because the seasoned nurse kept everything on schedule—including the surgeons, if need be.

Her back met the metal door before she stepped into the outstretched gown waiting in Baylee's hands. Once she was fully gowned and gloved, Sadie nodded to the room. "Let's start the time out."

"All right, folks. Confirming that this is patient Harold McMillan, right anterior superior iliac . . ."

◊◊◊

Three hours later, Sadie's back and feet were starting to ache. Filling a cup of water from the cooler in the OR interim area where surgical support staff would rest, relax, or eat between surgeries, she sank into a padded chair. The inevitability of tonight pricked at her right temple.

She warred with the duality of her thoughts. She loved Clark and meant what she'd said—that she didn't want to lose him. But she wasn't sure she'd be able to operate as a functioning person if she let loose everything inside her. She'd just learned that he desired her as much as she did him, but would he feel the same way after learning the depths of her sorrow?

Resting her elbows on the table, she settled the notch of her brows onto her steepled fingers. That slightly burnt scent from the electric cauterizer still clung to her skin, even though she'd been completely covered by either fabric or latex. Scrub techs passed by, laughing before they swiped their badges at the electronic clock beside the exit to the surgical wing. A deep breath filled her lungs as her head lifted to stare at OR 6.

The memory of the first time she'd been in that room at the early age of eighteen flashed through her mind. She'd been certain entering college on a full ride scholarship that she wanted to be a surgeon, so she'd applied for the pre-med program and joined the pre-med fraternity. Through an extension program, she'd shadowed a cardiothoracic surgeon, Dr. Strickland, several times during her freshman year.

The woman was incredible—barely five-two but a force to be reckoned with. Sadie shadowed with her as much as she could before the surgeon moved to chair a cardiothoracic program in Texas. Often, she'd taken Sadie aside after surgery to impart her wisdom.

"You're going to have to work twice as hard for half the result. They say equality in medicine is coming, but it sure as hell isn't here yet."

"Every day's going to be a trial. If you don't want to fight every day of your life, you should pick something other than surgery."

One day, after a particularly gruesome code and the death of the patient in OR 6, Dr. Strickland had bought Sadie a coffee, and they'd sat in the open courtyard.

The aroma of artisanally burnt beans mingled with the heavy scent of flowering lilac bushes.

"That one was rough. You okay?" Dr. Strickland asked.

"Yes, ma'am," Sadie replied automatically.

"Good." She nodded. "Some days will be like that. Some days nothing will go right, and everyone will die, but whatever you do, don't show vulnerability. Do it once and they'll walk all over you."

A stubborn smile laced her lips. "No need to worry about that, ma'am. I'm the youngest of three callous brothers and a disapproving mother. I stopped being vulnerable at age five."

Dr. Strickland grinned and paid her the highest compliment. "I think you're well suited for this, Miss Carmichael."

Sadie tore her eyes from the OR doors as her stomach twisted.

Now she *was* vulnerable. Vulnerability raced through her veins every day. Now she was the unhinged person who buried flower roots in the dark soil of various city parks because she couldn't bury her lost children.

Now she was the person who was pushing away the only person who'd *chosen* to love her because she couldn't see a way to open her mouth and let the waves of grief out without disintegrating entirely.

Now she was the person who couldn't even find refuge in the noisy hours of suction canisters running, machines beeping, and oxygen's gentle hiss in the background.

Her head fell into her hands again.

"Did someone die?"

Everything in her schooled instantaneously—her shoulders strengthened, her back firmed, her chin lifted to a resolute but not defiant position. "Not today."

"Ah, a good surgery day then." Her colleague Vinay settled himself in the chair opposite her. "Are you done for the day? I'd like to run through the resident schedule for July one last time. I had to change their shifts again to account for a new lecture series the medical school wants them to attend every Thursday."

She kept her face from flinching. The last thing she wanted to do was run schedules again; it felt like this was the thirtieth time they'd done this. But . . . it kept her from facing the unavoidable for another hour. "Sure. I can do that."

◊◊◊

Before she turned onto their street, Sadie paused for an extended time at the stop sign, rolling her neck like a boxer before a fight. Though Clark's words had been accommodating and understanding when she'd called and said she was going to be late coming home, his tone had alluded to something else.

Apprehension bounced inside her ribcage as she pushed her clogs into their wooden cubby and hung her keys. She had checked the woodshop first but hadn't found her husband there. Silently stalling, she'd run her fingers over his newest wall hanging designs—one that looked like a succulent plant in wooden form and another that resembled a magnified image of the veins of a leaf.

A full search of the house didn't reveal Clark's whereabouts, but the bolt to the backyard was unlocked. It'd rained today, though she hadn't been aware of it until after she pulled her car out of the employee garage, and the slick deck wet her socks. Clark's hunched form, sitting on the top deck stair, didn't stir. The faint yellow light from the wall sconce by the door dimly lit his profile as he stared out into the dark yard.

"I wasn't sure you'd be home before I went to sleep." His words held a slight edge.

"I'm sorry." Sadie settled herself on the same step, rainwater seeping through her scrub bottoms. "I'd rather have been here."

A rough derisive breath burst from her husband's body. "So you're saying that you weren't in the least bit relieved when Vinay sidetracked you after your last surgery?"

Her slight hesitation tore an expletive from his lips.

"This is never going to work if you'd rather be going through residency schedules than talking to your husband." His last two words were bit through closed teeth.

"I wasn't trying to avoid you tonight." That last modifier made the statement true. She hadn't been trying *tonight*. There had been many other nights when it'd been intentional, but Vinay had found her, not the other way around.

"Sure," he scoffed.

Her quads tensed, and before she recognized the action, she was standing, towering over her husband. Didn't he know how incredibly hard this was for her? Why was he making it worse?

Her hands gripped tightly at her sides as everything in her singed hot.

"Screw you, Clark."

Six distinct emotions ran across her husband's face before some manifestation of contempt remained. "Screw me? Isn't that what you've been doing? Screwing me and then leaving me? I guess I should be happy with that, right? That's what you're saying. I should take what I can get and be happy because God forbid I ask for something as simple as a conversation."

"I didn't say that. You're putting words in my mouth."

His jaw tightened before his gaze cast back over the grass. "At least someone is."

"That's not fair."

His eyes flicked back with a darkness that slapped her in the chest. "I don't think things have been fair for quite some time."

A sweeping tension coursed through her veins, telling her to run or fight or both. It was reminiscent of the handful of times one of her brothers had trapped her in a wrestling hold that she'd known was inescapable.

He shook his head. "You don't think I haven't noticed the change in your schedule? You don't think I haven't noticed that for the last week you've been home on time every day, and yet on the one night I need something from you, you get sidetracked? Tonight, you were supposed to put *us* first, to show me that I might actually mean something to you."

Her mouth dropped open with a wheeze as if he'd smacked her in the stomach. Of course, Clark meant everything to her. And they *were* going to talk; she'd just been delayed.

Clark only stiffened with her silence, punching to his feet. "Don't come upstairs. I'll toss some scrubs over the banister for your call tomorrow."

"Stop! You're being ridiculous." The shouted words were out of her mouth before she'd even considered them.

"I'm being ridiculous?" His nose almost brushed hers as his angry breath washed over her flushed face. "I've been nothing but patient and understanding with you, but I can't even get common courtesy back. I'm just—" He stepped back as his eyes darted around, looking at anything but her. "I'm done."

The finality of the word sliced through her. "Done?"

A muscle in his cheek twitched. "At least for tonight."

He stepped toward the house, and this impulsive panic overtook her. Rushing in front of him, she shoved his chest with her flattened palms. Only with her wet socks, she ended up sliding back several inches.

"Don't." His word was a growled warning.

For the first time in their relationship, touching her husband hurt her hands. Pain barbed through every contact point, ratcheting up her arms with a seizing sensation. An agonized inhale drew into her mouth as she yanked them back for inspection. In the seconds spent confirming her fingers weren't burnt or marred, her husband stormed into the house and slammed the door behind him.

·CHAPTER 24·

A grating, mechanical dying sound followed the unintentionally forceful slam of Clark's palm against his alarm. His quick glance revealed blacked out digital numbers of his now broken clock.

"Great. Just great."

He'd barely slept last night, thinking about his disagreement with Sadie. No, not a disagreement. It was an actual fight—the first one they'd ever had. A small, almost silent part of him whispered, *Good.* If they were shouting at each other at a decibel level that should have woken Lottie, at least words were being exchanged. It was strange to prefer that to silence, but that's what reverberated in his strained muscles this morning.

He shook his head before swinging his legs out of bed. Lottie was sleeping on her side on the monitor, her blanket balled at the bottom of the bed. His chest felt like a trigger clamp was ever tightening around it.

Since last night, he'd been playing a different mental game. The one where instead of telling himself everything was okay with Sadie being distant or physically absent, he'd told himself that he and Lottie would be okay after a separation. That it wouldn't break his heart every time he saw Sadie and couldn't hold her. That Lottie was young enough that having divorced parents wouldn't seem unusual because it would be all she could remember.

His eyes snapped back to the monitor as its rainbow volume bar illuminated across the top—Lottie was stirring. It only took a handful of steps to be at her bedside, rubbing her messy auburn curls.

"Dada." She smiled as her eyes opened.

"Hi, little love." His voice cracked, and he cleared his throat. "Ready to play with Omar?"

His daughter's little forehead wrinkled. "No! No stooler. Play with Mama."

Normally, he'd give Lottie the spiel he usually did when Sadie was working. One that he'd believed before—Mama did want to be with them, and as soon as she could, she'd be there.

Now those words rang hollow.

"I'm sorry." Defeat pushed down on his shoulders as he bowed over his daughter, pressing his forehead to hers. "I'm so sorry, Lottie."

"No!" Her little hands pushed his face away before she scooted herself out of her toddler bed.

Clark watched as if disembodied while she left through the open door, lavender bunny under one arm, searching for his wife. The echoed sounds of little feet and "Mama!" ricocheted off the walls of their empty house until at last the sound of Lottie crying jolted him back into his weary bones.

He doubted that any amount of exercise or parenting or distraction would be able to dissipate the ache settling in his chest this morning, but at least his sobbing daughter gave himself something to do. He couldn't soothe his own aguish, but he could try at least to comfort his child.

◇◇◇

"Did you get cut off in traffic on the way here or something?"

"What?" Clark glanced up from his inverted push up.

Victor was struggling to complete a set on the ground next to the picnic table that held Clark's feet. "You're just going extra hard today."

He grimaced. "Tough morning."

Lottie hadn't stopped crying, even when he'd bribed her with apple juice and pancakes. She'd sobbed the entire drive to the park and had been flailing in her five-point stroller restraints until Victor had rolled Omar next to her. Sometimes when Sadie had several days off and then returned to work, Lottie had a hard time adjusting to her mother's sudden absence, but this was the worst he'd ever seen. Even now, she was hiccuping, sucking the first two fingers on her left hand with moist eyes.

"I've got gummy snacks. Do you want me to give her a pack?"

"You can try," he said to the rough cement beneath his face. "She won't take anything from me."

In the background of his gritted exhales as he continued to pump himself away from the earth, he heard Victor's success in getting his daughter to eat something—a pack of gummies and a few graham crackers.

When he righted himself to move the kids to another section of the park, Clark said his thanks. Often, they stayed under the ramada, but when the kids were extra fussy, they did bodywork exercises and moved around the park to distract them. The last stop was by the dog park. They lined the strollers facing the various canines frolicking and chasing each other.

Once class was done, Clark tried to dust the grass off his T-shirt and gym shorts. Given that it was eighty-three degrees with almost one-hundred-percent humidity as it was forecasted to rain later, not much of the debris budged from his sweat-drenched clothes. He followed the rest of the dads back to the ramada, begging off extra time at the playground, and it wasn't until he'd crossed onto the pavement that Sadie stepped out from behind his slate grey truck.

Clark was pissed at himself for his reaction. His eyes automatically dragged over her faded denim cutoffs and snug white tank. So much of her lovely skin was showing.

"Hey," she stepped forward slowly, her right wrist flipping once.

"What are you doing here? Aren't you on call?"

Her eyes stayed on his—focused, insistent. "I found someone to finish it for me."

"Mama!" Lottie grunted and fought against her restraints again. "Down."

Sadie's gaze darted to their daughter before reaching forward and unbuckling Lottie. "Hi," she said, hugging their daughter and burying her nose in Lottie's neck.

The vision in front of him was all he truly wanted, but even as it was happening, he couldn't bring his tense shoulders down. "Why would you do that?"

A loud and controlled exhale left his wife's body. "Because I figured something out last night."

Unwittingly, he crossed his arms over his heart. "What did you figure out?"

"My way of communicating doesn't match yours." She shifted Lottie onto her hip. "You're good at saying things, expressing yourself. Which makes sense, your parents are the same way, always saying exactly what they're thinking. I can't do that. But . . . I want to show you something. Do you mind going on a walk with me?"

He hesitated, even though he felt the lift of his calves ready to step in whatever direction Sadie would lead them.

"Please." Some of that unmasked vulnerability flickered into the hollows of her cheeks.

A part of him wanted to be stubborn and insist she talk to him, but it was obvious she was trying in her own way, so a resigned "Lead the way" left his lips.

The ambient sounds of the busy public place in early summer were their only companions as she led him to the farthest corner of the park. The buzzing of the bugs mirrored his own vibrating anticipation of what to expect.

At last, they stood near the mulch bed of the lone sweetgum maple with three flower plants he'd seen the groundskeeper maintaining before. Sadie stared at the green of the plants—their tall, formerly petaled stalks bare.

"I'm not good with words. I work better with action. I think that's why I'm good at what I do. I have this need to physically fix things. I can't reason a bone back together—I need to do it manually." Her eyes lifted to his. "But I don't know how to do that with us."

His lips fell apart as a halting exhale left them.

Her gaze dropped to the plants again. "I have been avoiding you. Though I didn't intentionally do it last night, I've been doing it for months. Before or after work, I've been coming here and just"—she rolled her shoulders in discomfort—"sitting. It's been odd because I usually like movement, but I just sit. Sometimes in the grass. Sometimes on the top of a picnic table. I just sit, balled up for hours."

Fifteen different questions flew through his mind, but he was receiving his wish and sure as hell wasn't going to interrupt his wife when she was finally talking to him.

"And I think about them." Her voice cracked. "What would they have looked like? Would they like blackberry jam the best? What would be their favorite crayon to color with? Would they be calm and sleep through the night like this one"—she gently jostled a quiet Lottie—"or would they cry for hours, demanding they share our bed?" Her voice trailed off in a broken whisper.

"*Love.*"

Her eyes darted to his, and the anguish in them made everything in him seize. The roaring click of cicadas paused as vacant silence replaced all sound. Pain slowly rippled down his throat like he'd swallowed food without chewing it. It felt as if an immeasurable distance was expanding between them, though they stood a mere twenty inches apart. He half expected that when he reached his hand out to frame her face, his fingers would only grip the humid air.

When soft, supple skin pressed against the calloused pads on his fingertips, he heard his own startled breath break from his chest. She tilted her face to press her cheek into his hand, and a lone tear wet his palm. He couldn't recall the next sequence of events, only that he'd somehow managed to convince his daughter to favor the ground to his wife's hip so he could hold Sadie against him.

Clark expected her to break. To cry like she had in the shower after her third miscarriage, but instead she held him back with the same firmness he felt his muscles exerting. Their hearts thrummed within centimeters of each other, speaking silently to each other. Lottie kept her peace for about ten seconds before she began pulling on his shorts to a repetitive cadence of "up."

He knew he shouldn't ignore the life that had survived when Sadie had so heartbreakingly detailed her thoughts about the three that hadn't, but his wife was his only concern in that moment. His hand palmed the back of her head as he leaned back to bring her lips to his. As Sadie's soft kisses pressed against his mouth, an awareness broke over him—his wife showed her love physically.

A collage of images flashed through his mind—Sadie lovingly running her hand across various pieces of his craftsmanship; Sadie holding their daughter in her lap, on her hip, almost never setting her down; Sadie gripping him when they made love, never clutching the sheets or bed frame, but him—always him.

When a solid little fist met his thigh, he broke the series of closed mouth kisses with his wife and bent to pick up Lottie.

"I do it." Their daughter pecked Sadie's bare shoulder with slobbery lips.

His wife didn't laugh, but she ran her hand over their daughter's unbrushed hair as a small smile curved her mouth. When her gaze dropped to the plants near their feet, her lips downturned.

Suddenly, the strangeness of three plants at the base of a tree when he'd never seen that elsewhere in the well-manicured park made his stomach drop.

"Did you put these here?"

She nodded to the ground.

"Oh, love," he whispered, gathering his wife to his side.

Sadie was quiet for a long time before he heard her raspy words. "I'm sorry."

·CHAPTER 25·

"Love, you shouldn't be sorry for this."

The rebuttal to her husband's statement warred with Sadie's lips. If she argued and told him about the other parks with the other trios of flowers she'd planted, he'd see how unhinged she truly was. These three little plants were just the apex to a larger slab of impenetrable icy sorrow.

A novel flickering sensation jolted around in her body. She suddenly swelled with the need to unburden herself—to let words flow from her like blood from a wound.

But that was the problem.

Then she'd be bleeding without a surgical clamp in sight. Exsanguination would be the final result. With what she'd just told him, Sadie already felt as if she'd been skinned—more raw and exposed than ever before.

Her phone ringing in her back pocket pulled a relieved breath from her soundless mouth. Only when she saw her mother's contact on the screen, she winced. Her husband had a more decisive response, clicking the side of her phone to send the call to voicemail. "Not right now."

When her gaze flicked to his, he softened his tone and ran his hand up her arm. "You can talk to her later."

A second later his phone rang in his pocket. He shifted Lottie to his other hip to dig it out.

"Answer it," she said, seeing Penelope's contact on her husband's screen. "It's got to be something important if she's calling you."

Sadie's mind flew over all the possible reasons for her mother to call unexpectedly. Maybe she was ill or injured, or maybe one of her brothers was. Heart attacks weren't unheard of in forty-year-old men, and after the way Daddy had died, they were all at an increased risk. Her stomach bottomed out thinking maybe one of her adorable nieces or nephews had been in an accident. If they'd broken something, Sadie would want to oversee their care. How quickly could she get to them?

Clark frowned but slid his thumb over the screen. "Hello. Yes. She's—hold on."

She took the extended phone and pressed it to her ear. "What's wrong?"

"They're taking my car," her mother practically screeched. A male voice sounded in the background before her mother's muffled voice said, "Don't you have any manners? Just wait. I'm trying to sort it out with my daughter."

"Why are they taking your car?" Sadie squinted as the bright sun momentarily pierced between the densely gathered nimbostratus clouds.

"I don't know. Didn't you pay them for it?" Her mother's voice was more shrill than normal.

"No, Mama," she sighed, wiping sweat from her face. "That's what the money is for. I put it in your bank account, and then you make the payments. Haven't you been getting a bill from the dealership?"

A dismissive sound echoed over the phone. "I figured they were trying to charge me twice. Weasel what little money I had left from Daddy's life insurance." Sadie could tell that the last sentence wasn't for her benefit but for those around her mother. Penelope was probably dressed in her best shift, pressing her manicured hand to her waifish chest with pouty lips.

Sadie pinched her eyes closed. "Just tell them you'll pay them. That it's a misunderstanding."

A honeyed version of Sadie's words echoed in the distance followed by mumbled male voices and then her mother's trademarked "No need to be ugly" pointed at the men.

"They say they gotta take it, and I'll have to sort it out with the dealership."

"Okay, then that's what you've got to do, Mama."

"I don't need your sass," Penelope snapped. "It's not like you ever did anything right. Anything like you're supposed to. I don't even know why I called you. I should've called your brother. Alden'll fix this." The phone cut out.

Sadie didn't look up as the phone fell to her side but could feel Clark's unrelenting gaze on her face. Her husband had been understanding, if not encouraging, a few months ago when her mother had asked for a little bit of money to buy a new car.

Her family had always been comfortably middle class, but since Penelope had envisioned herself worthy of finer things even though she'd never worked a day in her life, her mother had quickly blown through Daddy's pension. Thanks to Penelope's excessive spending, her adult children were now bailing her out of financial ruin. Embarrassed, Sadie had left that detail out of the initial conversation with Clark. All he'd been aware of was that her widowed mother needed help.

"I can't believe her."

Sadie could feel his anger zap across the humid air molecules between them.

A noisy exhale left her lungs in response.

"I don't like when she talks to you like that." The protectiveness in her husband's words drew her gaze.

"She's blood," she said finally, her body suddenly feeling too heavy for her legs to carry.

Clark's free hand cradled her neck, bringing her forehead to his. "You're too good a person sometimes." His lips kissed her brow before releasing her.

She shrugged, layering on the armor she usually wore. "Being her daughter has had its advantages. I never flinched when my professors, attendings, or fellow surgeons tried to bully me out of my field over the years. And it wasn't like they didn't try. I witnessed more than one mental breakdown by a fellow medical student or colleague. But compared to my mother, their attacks always seemed like a drop in the bucket."

Her husband's smile was sad. "That's not an advantage from her, love. That's you being incredibly resilient." Clark gathered her free hand in his, interlacing their fingers. "You're one of the strongest people I know."

She tried to hinder her blush, but the flicker in her husband's eye told her he'd caught it.

A whispered, "God, I love you," flushed over the tender inside of her wrist before his hot lips brushed the skin.

Like the many times before when Clark had stunned her with his words, she didn't have a response. She wanted to wrap herself around him, to somehow be able to touch every part of him at once. Her squeezing his fingers seemed like a paltry substitute, but her husband didn't seem to mind.

A grin laced his face. "Do you want to get pancakes with us? We—"

"Pa-cakes!" Lottie interrupted with raised hands.

Her husband's surprised laugh at Lottie's interjection warmed and stirred something low in her belly.

"We didn't eat breakfast." He cleared his throat, his face sobering. "It was a rough morning." His expressive eyes told her he'd been struggling after their argument as much as she'd been.

She stepped closer, never relinquishing the stranglehold she had on Clark's hand. "It was really hard on me too."

Those words only held a tiny percentage of the agony Sadie had felt during the hours she'd spent in the guest room staring at the mahogany-bladed ceiling fan turning a lazy circle. By morning, she'd understood that if she didn't meet Clark where he stood, on his terms, she'd lose him forever.

Her collarbones itched with the knowledge that she'd only taken the smallest step toward letting him in—that she hadn't been brave enough to bare her whole soul to him. Maybe she could get there over time, but right now all her body craved was Clark's strength. Lottie's leg kept her from pressing her body to his, so she rubbed her daughter's back instead, closing the circle of the three of them like a circuit. Lottie flopped her head onto Clark's shoulder, sucking her fingers.

"Thank you for finding us"—his eyes flicked to the gerbera daisy plants—"and thank you for showing me this. For explaining why you've been distant, and why you've been gone so much. But I want you to know you're not alone. I'm right here with you. I—" His chest rose with a shaky inhale. "I'm having a really hard time too. Every time I stumble upon a baby toy in the playroom or see the newborns with their dads at class, I hurt too. I understand you wanted to deal with it alone, but maybe now we can work on it together?" Sorrow etched into the slight creases at the corners of his eyes.

The oppressive need to ease her husband's obvious suffering overthrew the twitchiness splintering throughout her muscles at the idea of opening herself up fully. "Yes."

Clark's eyes rounded slightly, but his voice was cautious. "And we can talk to someone about it? I really think we need help with this."

She swallowed over the saliva trying to drown her and nodded. "I might not do it right, but I'll try."

Maybe with time and the help of a professional, she could microdose her sorrow into the world. Maybe eventually, it wouldn't feel like each time she opened her mouth, her bones were crumbling.

The corner of his lips pulled up before he brought her knuckles to them. "Right now, that's all I need."

A wet popping sound accompanied Lottie tugging her fingers free. "Eat, eat. Dada say pa-cakes."

Clark dropped a kiss on their daughter's cheek. "I did say that."

Sadie tilted her head, quickly and gratefully shifting gears. "Oh. Let's go to that little diner on Main Street that puts Fruity Pebbles in the batter."

"An jooce! I want jooce."

"This one drives a hard bargain." He bounced Lottie, squeezing her thigh, and she giggled. "All right. Fruity Pebble pancakes *and* juice." Clark pinned Sadie with a teasing glare, his mouth forming his fully dimpled smile. "I hope you know she gets this commanding behavior from you."

Sadie opened her mouth, but her husband interrupted her with a kiss. It started soft, almost like a peck, but then he pushed further. Light streaked through her chest at the pressure of Clark's lips against hers. His face hovered millimeters from hers when he spoke. "I love that about her, and I love that about you."

·CHAPTER 26·

Sadie's beautiful ankle crossed over her knee before she nestled Lottie in the little crater she'd created with her legs atop his folding chair. Clark would be content to stand for hours if he got to gaze upon his wife beneath his canopy tent all morning. The weekend his parents had been visiting, he'd been nervous bringing Sadie to see what he'd been doing with his weekends, but now that they'd agreed to talk things out together, he wanted her here with him every Sunday.

"I never really got to see how this worked before," she said, seemingly reading his mind. "Is there anything I can do to help?"

His chest squeezed, but he kept his words even as he finished his setup. "Not really. We wait for people to come to us, answer questions, and cash out purchases. You can keep Lottie distracted. It's been busy the last couple of Sundays."

Sadie kissed their daughter's cheek. "That I can do."

The market was bustling today, and since Clark didn't have much time to chat with his family, Sadie offered to walk Lottie around. He'd be halfway through explaining which types of wood were in a piece to a customer and catch his wife's auburn ponytail in the distance chatting to Thatcher or another seller. Every time he caught a glimpse of her, his heart would stumble on its beat.

When they finally came back, Lottie held one of his wife's hands while the other held an agave lollipop. Since yesterday, he could almost see every action his wife had taken through a new light. Sadie trying to connect with the people in his life was her way of trying to stay connected to him.

Although the morning was already hot, he felt warmed from the inside out. "There are my loves."

Lottie ran over to him, holding up her lolly. "Look, Dada."

"You must have been visiting Miss Robin," he said, picking her up.

"She reminds me so much of your mom." Sadie pushed her sunglasses onto the top of her head.

A deep smile lifted his lips. He'd missed moments like this when he and Sadie had always been so in sync. "That's the first thing I thought when I met her."

This insecure look raced across Sadie's face before she tucked it away.

Quickly reading and understanding her expression, he added, "That's the *only* thing I thought."

"Really?" The question was more of a breath.

"Really." He settled his lips securely over hers.

His wife's hand rose to grip his bicep. The soft but passionate kiss was interrupted by Sadie's phone ringing in her back pocket.

She gave him a look of apology before she took a step away. "It's Linus. Just give me a minute."

His attention was diverted by another market patron for a few minutes before his brain started picking up the single side of his wife's phone conversation.

"It doesn't matter that I got my shift covered yesterday. Kerem was more than happy to finish it for me. That's why we have that system set up—to help each other out. Why does Josh even care?"

After her colleague's quick answer, she scoffed. "What? That's ridiculous. Reagan graduates in *two weeks*. She could have done the ORIF entirely on her own. Me stepping out while she closed is a nonissue."

His wife fell silent, listening to her colleague speak as he cashed out the middle-aged woman.

Lottie fussed on his hip. "Down. I want Mama."

"Not right now, little love. She's on a work call, give her a minute." His eyes watched Sadie stalk back and forth in the small space behind his tent, each turn of her sandaled foot becoming more aggressive than the last.

"I was late to one surgery. *One* morning. We've all slept through our alarms before. We're human. And I worked through lunch, so only the morning schedule was slightly behind."

Guilt twinged through Clark's belly right next to where his daughter's leg was impatiently wiggling, knowing he was the reason Sadie had been late that day.

"*Review board?* There's nothing to bring me up for."

Linus must have agreed with her because her ever-reddening face soothed as she stood still and listened for a long time.

Turning on her heel, she resumed pacing. "This is just because he doesn't have a life outside the OR—" She paused, nodding emphatically. "Right, you've got four kids, but he never came after you when Jonah was admitted with RSV and you rescheduled a week's worth of surgeries to be with him. The rest of us understood and helped you out."

She paused again and loosened the fingers that had been clenched into a fist. "Thank you for saying that." Sadie was silent before her head dipped sharply once. "Okay. Thanks for the heads up, Linus. I appreciate it."

Her finger punched the screen before she looked up with a forcefully blown breath.

No customers were nearby, so he said, "Let me guess? Josh is being a dick again and trying to get your job?"

"*Yes.*" His wife's hand gripped her phone as her jaw clenched. "A giant usurping dickhead. He's trying to build a case for my dismissal from directorship because I was late that day and I stepped out of surgery on another occasion."

"Can he do that?"

"No. Not really, but he can bring up the fact that I don't have a perfect record to the attention of the group. Which I suppose is his goal. Seed doubt, maybe? I don't know." She slammed her phone face down on the play table.

Lottie kicked and whimpered at his side chanting, "Mama." Sadie looked up with a long exhale and outstretched her arms. Clark was unsure if he should hand Lottie over, but when Sadie gathered their daughter to her chest, the anger that twisted her features seemed to dissipate. Her auburn lashes settled serenely on her cheeks as she inhaled their daughter's scent. The two most important people in his life tightly held each other while the humming noise of the market swept around them.

That swinging two by four to the chest sensation knocked the breath from his lungs. Everything fell away as realization dawned—before Lottie's accidental pregnancy, Sadie had mentioned not wanting kids. Though she clearly relished being their daughter's mother, maybe the only reason she kept trying after each miscarriage was because he'd always mentioned that he wanted two children.

A burning sensation flared beneath his breastbone as an agonizing resonance shot down his forearms and stung the pads of his fingers. Yesterday, Sadie had only given him a glimpse of how hard this year had been on her, revealing an ounce of suffering when she'd clearly been experiencing an ocean full. They should have had the conversation about stopping a long time ago, but his wife had been so insistent, and he'd been preoccupied with the idea of a sibling for Lottie.

But their daughter wasn't destined to have the childhood he had. The circumstances of each were entirely different. He had resources that his parents had never had. Plus, he was a different person than his father, who'd been a quiet introvert who hadn't really been interested in scheduling playdates for him. Lottie's two-and-a-half-year-old life was already filled with more playground sessions, swim lessons, and afternoon activities than he'd had in his entire childhood.

Again he hadn't protected his strong, determined wife when he should have. An apology was lacing his lips, vibrations almost resonating from his voice box, when Sadie's pale green eyes opened with a solemn expression.

"Maybe I should step down."

His wife's uncharacteristic words jolted him out of his own thoughts. "What? No." He moved so they were inches from each other. "There's no one—*no one*—more capable and deserving of this job than you. Let Josh choke on his own misogyny. The rest of your partners will be behind you, just like Linus." His hand framed her face. "You've worked too hard to get here. Don't let him ruin your accomplishments."

Her eyes darted away. "But maybe he has a point. I haven't been as focused on the job since"—she wiggled her shoulders—"everything." Her gaze settled back on his, almost begging him to understand something unsaid. "I've been kind of . . . crazy."

His brows twinged together. "What do you mean cr—"

A gentle cough sounded from behind him. "Excuse me, sir. How much is this one?"

Reluctantly, he turned and gave his attention to the older man standing on the other side of his display table. Over the next hour, he was bombarded by customers, but his eyes kept flitting to his wife, leaning almost in half on the folding chair so she could color with Lottie. He swallowed, watching her shading purple over blue. She always colored outside the lines on purpose so Lottie wouldn't feel bad about her own coloring ability. That compressed air feeling built up in his body again.

The plan had been to take Lottie out for lunch, but once they'd packed everything up, their daughter's sweaty pink cheek pinned her sock bunny against the side of her car seat as her mouth slacked open.

"I guess we're heading home." He gently closed the driver's side door.

Sadie nodded from beside him.

They both were quiet on the drive home. His muscles tightened, imagining the thoughts of inadequacy that might be running through Sadie's mind, and realizing that he was partly to blame for them. After he transferred Lottie into her bed for her nap, he found Sadie curled up on the small bench in their walk-in closet.

"I'm sorry," she whispered to her knees.

Tension squeezed at his throat as he collapsed next to her, gently rubbing circles over her arched spine. "For what? You have nothing to apologize for."

"I . . ." The words froze in her mouth, and she swallowed and tried again. "With the flowers. There's something I didn't . . . When I lost them . . . I thought it was okay, that I could keep everything separated, but I'm not handling it . . . I . . ." Her lips worked soundlessly again.

"*Sadie.*" He gathered her balled body against his. "I can't have this. I can't have you hurting like this because of me."

Her brows pinched as she raised her face.

A deep breath drew in before he swallowed. "I think we should stop—"

Sadie's phone rang from its position wedged between her body and the wall.

"Ugh." She closed her eyes, shifting to pull it from behind her.

He saw Kerem's smiling, professional headshot on the screen.

"I'm sorry, but I should take this." His wife's face slacked, holding the glowing, vibrating phone in her upturned palm.

Right now, Sadie was in the crossfire of Josh's asshole attempt at a power grab and needed to focus on that. They could talk about this tomorrow or in a few days. Maybe the best idea was to wait until they were in the presence of their new therapist to help Sadie process this change in his hopes for their family. All he knew was that there was no way in hell he was going to be the reason for his wife's pain.

He straightened his own features before leaning forward to kiss her forehead. "It's fine, love. We're okay. Deal with this."

"Thank you," she whispered to him before accepting the call in her normal authoritative voice. "Let me guess, you just received a call from Josh about my ability to lead."

·CHAPTER 27·

"Sorry I'm late." Sadie took her seat across from Parker at the high-top patio table, snagging a gulp from the short glass of ice water at her spot. "It's been a crappy week."

She'd texted Parker in all caps once things had settled down last Sunday, complaining about her colleague's attempt to bring to light . . . what? That she was human and had a life outside of surgery and sometimes needed to focus on that?

Fortunately, she'd received phone calls from several of her fellow surgeons, each giving her a heads up to Josh's plan. The fact that so many of them had called her in warning reinforced her confidence that she was still capable of handling the conflicts in her home life while still thriving at work. She hadn't crumbled yet. It was taking all of her energy, but she was still standing.

"I still cannot believe that slimy, underhanded son of a—"

"Evening, ladies. My name is Freya. Can I get you started with something other than water?"

As the young server wearing a crisp all-black uniform covered by a teal apron left the table, Sadie took a deep breath of outside air for the first time that day. The popular wine bar was a sought-out location any time of year, but now when all the various potted plants in old wine barrels were saturated with blooms atop on the multi-tiered stone patio, it looked like they were relaxing outside a villa in the Tuscan hills, not in downtown Durham. The only thing off about the ambiance was the nearby street noise.

Sadie's gaze flicked over the other well-dressed patrons and then down at her scrubs. "Sorry I didn't change. I've been so off, I only put a pair of slacks in my bag, but no blouse. I figured it'd be better to keep on my scrubs than wear slacks and a scrub top."

Parker waved a dismissive hand. "It doesn't matter what you wear. You've got Clark. I, on the other hand"—she gestured over her captivating fit-and-flare sundress—"have flies to catch."

Her lips downturned. "What happened with Ivan?"

Parker spread her hands on top of the wine barrel lid turned tabletop. "Things didn't pan out."

Since their relationship had never really been based on the sharing of their emotions, Sadie let the moment pass without digging for more information. Soft acoustic guitar music floated into the space she'd left open.

"Bronze Hills Pinot Noir and the Sunkissed Cab," Freya said, setting down their glasses of wine. "Can I get you ladies anything to snack on? A charcuterie board or some bruschetta?"

"This is fine for now. Thank you," Parker answered before taking a large gulp of her glass of cabernet.

As soon as their server left, Sadie opened her mouth to offer a surgical story as a distraction, but Parker interrupted her.

"Do you have any idea—*any idea*—how rare men like Clark are? How rare it is to have a man who accepts a woman who works like we do?" A humorless laugh fell from her mouth. "I mean, that was always our goal, right? Fight for equality in our fields. Constantly battle jackasses like Josh who never stop trying to take us down. And then on top of all of that try to find someone who doesn't mind our crazy schedules and actually *wants* a strong, independent woman."

Parker's fingers spun her wine glass by the stem, and rivulets sloshed dangerously close to the rim. "Because they'll swear up and down that they want an independent woman. Someone who doesn't need them, but it's all a bunch of lies. They don't. They might for a night or maybe a few weeks, but that's it. It never lasts. The only time I've ever seen it work is with you."

Sadie nearly toppled off her backless stool she reared back so quickly from her friend's frustrated glare.

"You've seemed to find the *one man* on the planet who not only doesn't mind but happily puts his career on hold and raises Lottie while you get to do what you love all day. Do you have any idea how freaking rare that is?" Fellow patrons looked over as the volume of her voice climbed.

Parker's eyes widened before her face fell in her hands with a groan. "I'm sorry. I'm being a shitty friend. I know you've been through hell this year, and you've had to deal with Josh all week, and now I'm"—an exhale punched from her as she brought her gaze up—"I'm just jealous. I have been for a long time."

Sadie could feel her brows twinging as words burst from her mouth. "But you're the one who told me to kiss Clark in the first place."

Her friend groaned again. "I know, but I thought you'd have one night of steamy sex with someone who was actually hot instead of the sparse and sad interactions with the losers you usually went out with. I didn't think you'd find *your person*."

Sadie's mouth opened to formulate words, but her jaw worked soundlessly.

Parker took a noisy inhale. "It's just at the end of the day, you're not alone. You've got a husband—a partner—who would bend over backwards to give you what you need. I just—it'd be nice. Just once, you know? I'm supposed to be tough and not need anyone, but after watching you and Clark, I thought maybe it could happen for me too." Her gaze dropped to the tabletop. "I really thought it was going to work out this time. I thought maybe Ivan was my person."

Clarity hit Sadie like an orthopedic hammer to the temple. It *was* incredibly rare what she and Clark had. And she'd spent the year selfishly trying to sort through her own grief without considering his. At the park, he'd said it had been hard on him, but even in that moment, she hadn't offered solidarity, hadn't supported him. She'd only worried about how hard it was for her to open up. If she kept going on like this, keeping everything inside, her marriage would be over.

Adrenaline surged through her body until it felt like the fine hairs on her arms were burning. She needed to show Clark the rest of the flowers. She had to be completely honest with him. And then she needed to make space inside herself to take in *his emotions*—his fears, grief, worries. Clark had always been so affable and capable, she'd never considered having to support him, but he was as much of a bereaved parent as she was. He needed Sadie to be better—to listen and commiserate and to be capable of taking on his emotional burden.

Much like Parker did right now. Her courageous friend was in pain and needed her support.

Sadie quickly covered her friend's hand with her own. "I'm sorry things didn't work out with Ivan." She paused to swallow her discomfort. "Why don't you tell me what happened?"

Parker gripped Sadie's hand while the other one brought the remaining gulp in her glass to her lips. "No. I've already been too much of an ass with my outburst. I'll be okay. I always am."

She squeezed her fingers. "You don't have to be, you know?"

"Yeah. Yeah." The winking orange tabby inked over Parker's right shoulder bounced as her friend's gaze skirted to the side. "Can we focus on something else?"

"No." Sadie surprised herself with her answer. Her brain had already been ready with an affirmative response and a distracting surgical story. "I mean, I think it will be better—that you'll feel better—if we talk about it. Just a little bit."

Parker tugged on a long strand of hair in front of the barely-there straps of her dress, and Sadie's chest ached watching her friend struggle with her words. So many times that had been her.

"I just—I think I'm ready for something else. Dating Ivan wasn't like all the other quick and casual relationships I usually engage in. I tried to be"—her eyes focused on the potted plants behind Sadie's shoulder—"more me. I figured it worked for you, why not try it?"

Sadie nodded, not sure if she should just listen or try to say something.

"But it didn't work out. And because I didn't keep my cards close, I've had this naked feeling following me around all week." Her friend offered a weak grin. "I know I usually walk around half-naked, so you'd think I'd be used to it."

A sympathetic expression pulled at Sadie's face. "I know what you mean. When I finally told Clark how hard this year has been on me, I felt like someone had stolen my skin and all my organs were on display."

"Is that enough talking?" Parker fiddled with her empty glass. "I've heard the phrase 'sharing is caring,' but I was hoping that would apply more to appetizers than my innermost workings."

Sadie almost snorted her wine but managed to swallow the liquid a second before their server arrived to check on them.

After they ordered a variety of items, Sadie leaned back on her stool, her brain reeling with the right thing to say. "Since you're catching flies, do you want me to be your wingwoman tonight? I can run home and change into that ridiculous dress you made me buy."

Parker's lips lifted in a woeful smile. "I must really be a train wreck if you're offering to wear a dress for me."

The bold flavor of the wine burned the top of Sadie's throat. "I'm sorry. I was trying to make you feel better, but I suck at this."

A chuckle burst from her friend. "No more than I do. We are two bumbling toddlers here. Honestly, I'd love it so much right now if a car would jump the curb and drive into the side of the restaurant to give us a chance to show our strengths. Because this talking nonsense is crap."

Unexpected laughter overtook Sadie so swiftly that a sheen of tears tugged at the edges of her vision, threatening to fall freely to the lacquered table-top.

"Imagine it." Parker spread her hands wide in front of her chest, her eyes lit up. "Boom. Crash. Is there a doctor in the house? And then we run to the rescue. *God*, wouldn't that be nice? You wouldn't even have to worry about trying to get blood out of your clothes later. You're already in scrubs."

Honestly, that sounded like heaven.

"Are we bad people for wanting that right now?"

Parker snorted. "No. We're emotionally stunted adrenaline junkies, maybe, but not bad." She looked longingly at the traffic flying by the restaurant patio. "How'd Clark like that dress, by the way? I never asked."

Distracted by the idea of setting bones in the field, her cheeks pinked before she could stop them.

A devious twist lifted one side of Parker's mouth. "Uh-huh. That's what I thought. You should wear it to graduation tomorrow."

Sadie folded her arms, intentionally cooling her face. "It's a professional event. I'm wearing a pantsuit."

"Fine." Parker rolled her eyes before they rested on her water glass and her shoulders drooped. "Actually, do you think it would be okay if I watched Lottie tomorrow? I know it's been a while, but I think I need a change of pace. The bar scene is obviously not working for me right now. I think it might"—she looked up—"be good for me."

"Of course. Lottie would love that."

"And *bonus*, your daughter can only string a few words together, so she won't require much from me verbally."

Sadie found herself laughing again. "That's true."

"It's settled, then." The tension in Parker's jaw seemed to loosen as she leaned her elbows on the table. "Did I tell you about the amature MMA fighter I treated on Tuesday?"

The corner of her mouth kicked up. "No. No, you didn't."

·CHAPTER 28·

"Poison control and all the emergency numbers are on the fridge." Clark ran a hand through his hair before remembering he'd styled it with pomade.

"Clark, relax. I *am* the emergency response, remember? I know it's been a while since I've watched her, but we got this, don't we Lottie?" Parker held her free hand up for a high five. Her other hand was securely wrapped around his daughter's waist, keeping her on Parker's romper covered hip.

Lottie stopped tracing the pumpkin vines on Parker's forearm and slapped her little fingers to Parker's. "Yeah!"

He was about to run through Lottie's bedtime routine again when Sadie breezed into the kitchen. Her hair was down, falling in waves over the jacket of her light grey pantsuit.

"Ready?"

"Yeah," he breathed once the air returned to his lungs again.

After goodbye kisses for Lottie, they paused in the mudroom for Sadie to slip on her flats. He jogged around to the passenger side of his truck to open the door before Sadie pulled it open herself.

His wife paused before getting in. "You look really nice tonight." Her hand ran the button line of his navy collared shirt underneath his open black suit jacket. Seemingly unsatisfied, her fingers raised again, fidgeting with the knot of his black tie.

"You too." The words hoarsely left his lips.

Her eyes flicked to his as her mouth parted slightly. He was leaning in when the garage door flung open.

"Bye bye!" Their daughter waved enthusiastically.

"*Okay.*" Parker ran into the door frame. "She's definitely gotten faster in the last couple of months."

A strangled sound broke from his throat, but Sadie only smiled as she stepped into the cab of his truck. "Have a good time, you two."

◊◊◊

After a short ceremony congratulating each resident and the giving away of various accolades, everyone gathered around the dining tables of the second-story private room of the swanky restaurant. Overlapping conversations bounced around the room as people drank their cocktails and gathered plates from the various food stations.

Not every attending surgeon in the group was there, but since his wife was the director, she and a few others who worked more closely with the residents were. He'd recognized some of her colleagues' faces and was introduced to those he hadn't met before the simple ceremony started. Five residents had graduated this year including Sadie's favorite, Reagan. His wife was incredibly excited that Reagan had decided to take an offer with their surgical group and stay in Durham.

As Sadie moved around the room, congratulating each resident in turn, Clark collected another plate of delicious morsels. Even as he was placing asparagus wrapped in prosciutto on his plate, he couldn't help watching his gorgeous wife. She'd discarded her light grey blazer, and her skin seemed to glow from beneath her silky white sleeveless blouse.

"Where's that sweetheart of yours?" Maggie, the surgery practice's office manager, asked from behind him, holding an empty plate.

"A friend is watching her tonight."

"That's nice." She smiled, picking up a spoonful of lobster mac'n'cheese. "It's good for parents to get out by themselves every once in a while. I bet since your daughter is getting older, you two have been able to get out a bit more."

"Yeah, it's been nice," he lied. He and Sadie still had a lot of emotional space between them to recover, but he hoped regular date nights would come back into their life soon.

Maggie placed two rolls on her plate, continuing on. "How are all the projects on the house going? Sadie says you're always improving something."

A pleasant resonance settled just beneath his breastbone. Sadie wasn't the type to share unnecessary information or engage in small talk. If Maggie knew about his work at home, then his wife must have cared enough to discuss it on her own terms.

His eyes found Sadie again standing beside three colleagues. Clark could tell by the movement of her hands that she was detailing a surgery. That excited glow hovered around her, making her so beautiful he had to resist the urge to cover his pounding heart with his palm.

"I usually have a project underway."

"Since she's been picking up so many extra call shifts and scheduling those extra surgeries, it must be an expensive project."

That gut-punch sensation ripped away all his elation. He'd suspected Sadie had been picking up shifts, but it still hurt hearing it from Maggie.

Maggie patted his jacketed arm. "At least you've still got most of your Sundays together. I like that she made Sundays off a contingency of her accepting the directorship. It's important to have work-life balance. Few surgeons understand that."

The hairs on the back of Clark's neck stood up, and he rolled his shoulders to try and dissipate the sudden pinprick sensation. Somehow, he forced his feet to move down the table of food. Sadie still had Sundays off? Up until a week ago, she'd implied that she'd been on call or had been at mandatory meetings all those days. If she hadn't been at the hospital . . .

His gaze darted up.

Sadie pushed Vinay's jacketed arm as she, Linus, and Kerem burst into laughter. Clark blinked. Did her fingers linger? A sinking feeling pulled his stomach down to his calves. When he'd been introduced to the man before the graduation program started an hour ago, Clark hadn't thought anything about him. He was just another one of Sadie's many male colleagues. Now, however, he noticed Vinay was actually a rather attractive man. One who was smiling with rapt attention as Sadie spoke.

Apparently, Maggie had kept talking. ". . . makes sense because they spend so many years working to get to where they are, it's hard to take some time off."

"Uh, yeah, I'm sure you're right," he muttered. "It was good to see you. Excuse me." He moved away swiftly, setting his full plate on a nearby open table and walking out the side door that led to an exterior balcony.

Raspy loud breaths pulled into his lungs as his fingers found the notch between his brows. When the first miscarriage had happened and Sadie had become more emotionally distant, when the work hours had started to increase, he'd never even considered she wasn't in the OR. He'd always trusted her.

Even when she'd explained that she'd been mourning at the park, that had made sense to him. But considering that she might have been spending her free time with another man made his muscles revolt. They didn't know if they should loosen and drop him to the decking below his feet or tighten to the point of sending the bones of his fist colliding into the jaw of another man.

Clark glanced back through the plate glass window to see Sadie's smiling face pay more attention to Vinay than she did the other two men at her side.

Things started to click together like Lottie's chunky Duplo blocks. Sadie had said she'd been at Peaceably Park, but there were times when she would have been there at the same time he and Lottie were there for class or for an afternoon playdate on the playground. The park wasn't that big. He'd have seen her or her car. No, there were *definitely* times when she was scheduled off and he was at the park and she wasn't.

This plummeting sensation ripped through him, prompting his hand to grab the sun-warmed railing in front of him. He pulled his phone from his suit jacket pocket—6:46 p.m. Before the plan was fully formed in his mind, he was pushing back into the luxuriously decorated dining space.

Though his pulse was pounding in his throat and adrenaline was coursing through his veins, he made his mouth form an approachable smile as he interrupted the foursome. "Parker called. Lottie wants to say goodnight to us." He forced his fingers to not shatter the phone in his hand as he tilted his head toward the staircase that led back to the rest of the restaurant.

Sadie frowned slightly, and sourness hit the back of his mouth with a potency that was almost agonizing. She excused herself from the conversation before following him downstairs. He wasn't listening as Sadie babbled on about how excited she was that another particularly skilled resident had decided to join their practice as well. She didn't even seem to notice that he'd marched them out the front door and around the side of the restaurant where they could have some privacy.

At last, he turned and faced his wife. "Are you having an affair?" He'd planned on starting in a better, more clever way, but his brain only wanted an answer to that question.

"What? No!" His wife's brow pinched as her face morphed in shock. "Why would you ask that?"

Clark carefully gauged her reaction. He'd never thought of Sadie as a dishonest person, but maybe in the end, he really didn't know her. She kept so much to herself.

He crossed his arms across his chest to offer some protection to the organ breaking beneath his breastbone. "You admitted that you weren't working all the times you were away from home. That you were at the park thinking about our unborn children." He tried and failed to say the last sentence without his voice breaking. "But that can't be right, Sadie. There were times when we would have been there at the same time."

His wife's face froze, and that action was all he needed to see. An expletive left his lips as his eyelids closed painfully. She'd been lying to him. She'd told him she was grieving, but she'd been taking hours upon hours of time doing *something* away from him and Lottie.

"Have you been with him?" His arm swung to the restaurant.

"Who?"

"Vinay." Forcing himself to say the man's name almost made him vomit in his throat.

"No. I mean, not unless I said I was when we were working. But only working. Not doing anything else. Not doing what you think we were." She visibly shuddered, and he didn't know if he should take that as a good response or good acting.

"I put up with a lot. You not talking to me, pulling away, not wanting to work on our relationship, but I will not tolerate you sleeping with another man." His fingernails dug into his palm.

"I'm—" she sputtered. "I'm not. I promise."

"Then where have you been?"

"At the park," she said softly. "Ours and some other ones."

"After everything we've been through, you could at least be honest with me." He shook his head, stepping past her toward the parking lot.

"Clark, wait." She reached out and grabbed his forearm.

"Don't touch me." The wrenching back of his arm threw her off balance, but he didn't reach out to catch her.

She recovered her step. "I *am* being honest. I'm not having an affair." Her voice raised to near yelling. "I can explain everything. I was going to show you tonight after dinner."

Itchiness ran under his dress clothes, and he wanted to rip them off. "I don't even know if I can believe you now."

"Why not?" Her question was strained.

"Because you've obviously been lying, so why not lie about this too?"

Her eyes watered as her jaw worked soundlessly, and part of him *almost* gave in—almost wrapped her in his arms.

"I need to go. I can't"—he averted his eyes—"I can't look at you right now."

Sadie was wordless as her white ballet flats took a timid step back.

"I think," he said to the sidewalk below his feet, "maybe you shouldn't come home tonight."

He heard the way his words hit her, heard her pained breath before her objection. "But we're supposed to have a family day tomorrow after the farmer's market. It's Sunday. Lottie will miss me."

The fact that she'd brought up the one day that was supposed to be his made everything in him streak aggressively hot. Later, he'd rationalize his words as fair because at that moment he'd been too wrecked not to try and even the score by lashing out.

"Honestly, she probably won't even notice. You're so rarely home. Wherever you've been going to escape us, you can go there tomorrow."

·CHAPTER 29·

Sadie numbly watched her husband stalk to his truck, hugging her arms around her gnarled stomach. Tears tugged at the corners of her eyes, stinging the bridge of her nose and threatening to relinquish themselves to gravity. They wouldn't have even had this argument if she'd been strong enough to drive him to Lake Trail Park or any of the other parks last Saturday instead of taking the easy way out and joining him and Lottie for pancakes.

Her chest wouldn't feel ripped to shreds if she'd let herself bleed in front of him. If she trusted that he'd still want to wrap his arms around her and tell her he loved her. If she believed that the darkness inside of her wasn't so all-consuming that they couldn't survive it.

If she believed in *them*.

Cool determination settled over her flushed skin before she realized she was moving. All her muscles coordinated to sprint across the parking lot. Only, in the second row of cars, a shiny red Lamborghini screeched to a halt inches before cutting her down at the knees. Her eyes darted to the sleek sports car briefly before flicking back up to Clark's exiting truck pulling onto the street.

She pivoted, ready to run back into the restaurant to grab her phone where she'd left it in her suit jacket pocket when a familiar voice caught her.

"*Dr. Carmichael.* You of all people should know to be more careful. I could have easily broken your leg."

Josh's cropped blond head stuck out of the open window of the Lamborghini, a smug smile tugging at his lips. Beside him, a gorgeous black-haired woman was typing on her phone, ignoring their interaction.

Every single cell in Sadie's body wanted to scream at this man. If the daily emotional strain of trying to swim upriver wasn't enough, after a year of loss and an ever-fraying relationship with her husband, her strength was splintering. A visceral part of her wanted to kick the hood of his car like the supposed insane person she'd been telling herself she was.

Only . . .

Staring down at this chauvinist jerk, who was going out of his way to make things harder on her, her actions seemed guilelessly benign.

How she had responded to the trauma of losing her unborn children wasn't crazy. It might not have been the most healthy—spending time in the depths of gut-wrenching grief alone, unintentionally beautifying Northwood—but it didn't make her mentally unstable. It had been how she'd responded to insurmountable pain in a vulnerable state.

The only thing that mattered right now was explaining that to Clark—showing him where she'd been and what she'd done. The plan had been to make a few detours on the way home after dinner, but now she needed to go home and convince him to come with her. Her spine straightened as her shoulders took their usual stance.

If there was one thing she excelled at, it was tenacity.

Clark would understand once she explained everything. He had to.

An intentional, deep breath pulled into her lungs as she stepped out of the way of the car. "Dr. Arnold, it's nice to see you spending some time *outside* of the OR for once. Excuse me."

Sadie didn't wait for a response as she turned and strode back into the restaurant. She made quick excuses before being back in the parking lot minutes later. Looking for the blue sedan she'd called to take her home, she noticed Josh's flashy Lamborghini parked up front by the valet—with one of its tires completely flat.

This hyena-like laugh overtook her body before hearing her name being called from twenty feet away. In the hired car, the momentary reprieve she'd been given by seeing Josh get his cosmic comeuppance by way of a flat tire evaporated as the miles to her house decreased. Tension twined down the rod of her spine, seizing to a point of pain when her phone rang with Parker's number.

"Sadie, what happened? Where are you? Clark barely spoke to me, except to thank me for watching Lottie. He basically handed me my keys and shoes and shoved me out the door. What's going on?"

The exhale that left her mouth took a large portion of her strength with it. "I screwed up."

"But you're going to fix it?" The worried sound of her friend's voice unnerved her.

"Yes." She forced determination to infiltrate her words. "Yes. That's what I'm good at. Do me a favor, can you not leave the neighborhood? I'll need you to go back and be at the house and watch Lottie so I can take Clark somewhere. I need to show him something tonight."

"Sure. Whatever you need."

A few minutes later, she waved to Parker from her parked spot at the entrance to the neighborhood and thanked the driver when he dropped her in her driveway. Since Parker had mentioned that Lottie had already been put to bed before Clark showed up, Sadie didn't knock or ring the doorbell. Her incessant calls and text messages had gone unanswered, but she knew that there was a spare key tucked under the eave of the playhouse.

The grass bent and tickled the tops of her feet as her deliberate strides brought her across the backyard. A red breasted robin swooped low, snagging something from the grass before darting back to the tree line. Her momentum only halted when Clark's sharp voice startled her.

"I asked you not to come home."

He was seated at his usual spot on the top deck stair, his face tilted sideways as if he was trying not to look at her. He'd discarded his jacket, tie, and collared shirt, leaving only a snug grey undershirt untucked over his black slacks. The evening sun illuminated his clenched jaw line at such a sharp angle it made her blink.

"I know." She took a tentative step in the direction of the deck. "But I want to talk. I can explain everything. I just need to show you—"

"You don't get it, do you?" Clark punched to his feet, pinching the bridge of his nose. "I don't want to talk to you now. I told you not to come home, but here you are because in the end, it doesn't matter what *I* want. Everything's on Sadie's schedule."

She winced at his forceful words. The warm evening light flooding their backyard suddenly felt jagged and blinding.

"*You've* decided that you want to talk. *You've* decided it's time to work through things. What about what I want?" He stabbed his chest with a jerky hand. "We're supposed to be a team, Sadie. We're both supposed to matter in this. You're not the only one suffering. I mean, have you even considered how isolating this year has been for me?"

Tightness constricted her throat until only a desperate rasp escaped because she hadn't.

She hadn't considered his feelings, his sorrow, his solitude when going through her own. Over and over again, she'd distanced herself from him instead of reaching out. She'd behaved the way her mother had always told her she would. *She'd been selfish.*

Both hands flew through his hair as pain streaked over his face. "I can't live like this anymore. I can't be waiting for you to decide to choose me—to choose our family—and be disappointed time and time again when you don't. Lottie and I deserve more. We deserve to be more than an afterthought."

Sadie's mind raced like debris whipping through a tornado. Her impulse was to work until the shattered parts of her marriage were repaired so this disintegrating feeling would leave her muscles. But if she ignored Clark's words, if she pushed her agenda, she'd lose him. She wasn't sure she hadn't lost him already.

"Just—" She swallowed over the bile climbing her esophagus. "Just tell me what to do."

Clark rotated toward her, and the wetness shining in her husband's eyes made her whole body clench.

"I—I need some time to sort all this out." His shaky hands jammed into his pants pockets. "I think you should go."

Spots flashed over Sadie's vision as her body staggered back a step. Suddenly, the sight of the back of her house, something she'd seen hundreds of times, looked foreign. She wouldn't be entering its cozy walls tonight. Depending on what her husband decided, she might not enter with it feeling like home ever again. Her fingers wove wildly over her chest, trying and failing to subdue the suffocating sensation making her panic.

The only thing louder than the sound of her blood rushing in her ears was the voice that whispered, *You can't fix this. It's too late.*

Clark's gaze darted to the composite boards beneath him. "You can go in and gather a bag if you'd like. I'll wait out here."

"No," she rasped, taking a reflexive step back as if his words had physically shoved her. "That's okay."

Tomorrow when she wasn't falling apart, she'd worry about practical things like her car keys, a change of clothes, and toiletries. If she entered their home right now, not knowing whether or not she'd ever be welcomed back, she'd collapse.

Clark nodded, never raising his gaze.

Sadie wasn't sure how she managed, but somehow her feet carried down the driveway. She was halfway down her street when Parker's text sounded from inside her sweat-covered jacket.

Parker: *Should I come back?*

A sob tore from her throat as she responded.

Sadie: *No. Can I stay with you tonight?*

She didn't register the sound of her friend's car accelerating toward her, only knew that somehow Parker's inked arms were holding her upright before they buckled her limp body into the passenger seat. The drive to the townhouse complex where she used to live prior to buying her home with Clark happened in the span of one languid blink.

Then they were passing it. Eight twenty-nine. The little two-story, two-bedroom where she'd brought a handsy Clark that first night. They'd barely made it through her front door before an inverse of what had happened in Parker's garage occurred. The metal rim peephole had scratched her neck when he'd lifted her and pressed her against it with one arm.

Sadie's trembling fingers found the spinous process of her cervical spine. When her clammy hand gripped the back of her neck, everything left her. Tears were on her face streaming onto the leather seats of her friend's car, her muscles refused to hold their position as she sagged, the last of the oxygen in her body escaped, and she was sure—absolutely sure—she was bleeding to death.

She'd gone through the year from hell, losing life after life, but now she'd finally lost her husband.

·CHAPTER 30·

A slap echoed in the concrete-walled back area of Nash's Hardware Store as Clark set two more pine boards upon his stack. Nash's didn't have a wide wood selection, but the idea of spending the time he was paying Aurelia driving sixty minutes round trip to the lumber yard felt like a waste. He needed this time to complete a few more pieces to replenish the inventory he'd sold this morning.

Even though it'd rained off and on at the farmer's market, that hadn't deterred customers from nearly buying him out. Now that he had an hour gap in the day-long projected rainstorm, he wanted to get this wood home before it was soaked through. He was stacking another board into his cart when his phone pinged with a text. Had Lottie been with him, he would have ignored it, but since the message could be from Aurelia, he pulled the phone from the front pocket of his shorts.

Unlisted: *A reminder that your apt is at 9:00am tomorrow. Durham Psychological Services. Text STOP to opt out.*

Clark's shoulders pulled so far forward his muscles protested the action. He'd have to call the office first thing tomorrow and cancel. Though he'd championed them working with a therapist—finding one that specializes in pregnancy loss—even though Sadie had wanted to hash out everything last night, a part of him wasn't sure things could be fixed at this point. Coming home from the market today and finding her car, scrubs, and toothbrush gone had been a nail gun to the stomach.

"You told her to leave," he reminded himself.

After navigating the industrial panel cart around a revolving seed display, a ready-to-buy chicken coop, and a mess of hanging wind chimes, he stopped third in line at the register. To the left sat a folding table covered with plastic potted plants. Their viridescent rippled leaves resembled the plants Sadie had showed him at Peaceably Park last weekend. A pinprick tingling sensation swept his chest and traversed down his arms. When he looked back up, Buddy, the elderly store owner, had replaced the teenager at the register and the line had vanished.

"Clark! Good to see you." The older man adjusted the suspenders over his blue-striped collared Nash's Hardware shirt.

"You too." He clasped the man's outstretched hand.

"Haven't seen you in a while."

He shrugged. "Been working off my surplus, but it was time to get some more wood."

Buddy gave an *mmm-hmm* and started keying in the codes for the various boards Clark had stacked on the cart.

"Tell your wife we've got those flowers she's so fond of half-off through Sunday." A weathered, arthritic finger pointed to the gathering of white, yellow, and red flowers Clark had just been examining. "I always thought it was peculiar that she bought so many one at a time." He darted his eyes to the side before continuing in a stage whisper. "Not that you don't already know, being her husband and all, but she's an intense kind of lady, so I wasn't about to question her gardening methods. Not after she put Alice's hip back together so nicely five years ago." He punched a final button. "With your discount, that'll be $168.52."

Clark's fingers were numb as they fumbled for his credit card and pushed it into the card receiver. "You know, she spread them all around. I feel like I don't even get to see half of them. How many did you say she bought?"

The man's thick grey brows rushed together.

"We're on one of those five acre lots." The lie felt like sawdust in his mouth, but his need to know the answer weighed on him more than the unease of being dishonest.

"Ah." He tilted his head back, thinking. "I'd say about twenty-five or so, maybe more."

Clark barely stifled the sharp cough that wanted to escape his lips.

Buddy ripped the receipt off the register and handed it over. "Good luck with your project. Tell the missus 'hi' for me."

Some mumbled appropriate salutation was created by his throat, but he didn't register his movement away from the counter and through the automated exit doors until his cart was stalled beside the tailgate of his truck.

Twenty-five.

His mind quickly ran through the calculation, dividing that number by three. He moved forward unseeing, scratching his shin on the edge of a wood board. The pain brought back his faculties, allowing him to load his truck and find himself behind its idling wheel, hand frozen on the gear shift. He pulled his phone out of his front pocket and did a quick search of local parks. There were dozens within several smiles. Bruised storm clouds threatened to open up again as he clicked his GPS to navigate.

The next closest one, with the exception of Peaceably Park, was the one with the baseball and soccer fields. It was more of a field park than one meant for picnics and playtime, which was why he'd never brought Lottie here. Once his truck screeched to a stop in the parking lot, he jogged around the perimeter and was mentally calling himself a crazy man until he caught a glimpse of white in front of the kudzu-covered trees beyond the last outfield.

His heart galloped against his breastbone when he skidded to a halt in front of it, his hands finding his knees. Only half of the slim white petals were still attached to its dark center. The plants bookending the center one held only bare stalks. They were undeniably the same ones he'd seen at Nash's Hardware Store—the same ones Sadie had shown him.

Even though she'd denied having an affair last night, Clark hadn't been able to relinquish his suspicion that she couldn't have spent all that time alone. But staring at an exact replica of the arrangement she'd planted at Peaceably Park, one thought ricocheted in his skull.

She'd been telling the truth.

A sweaty palm ran the length of his chest before his calves clenched to race back to his truck. Sadie's phone rang to her voicemail twice, and he pitched his phone on the passenger seat before realizing that maybe he could find her this way. He tapped into his GPS again.

After two more confirmations and one misfire, he pulled into the gravel parking lot of Lake Trail Park beside his wife's crossover. Having found her, he expected himself to bolt from his truck and run like he had before, but instead, his limbs felt filled with wet concrete as he stumbled onto the tiny rocks at his feet.

His eyes flowed over the ramada and bathroom. When he came up empty, he stepped to the trailhead to the circular path, said a silent prayer, and turned right. Soft, rain-saturated mulch compressed soundlessly beneath his work boots. After about a quarter-mile, a glimpse of dampened auburn hair flickered to the left of the trail.

A small clearing in the trees and brush was occupied by a fallen log some enterprising hiker had placed parallel to the water as a perch to gaze upon the lake. Sadie sat atop it, wet yellow T-shirt suctioned to her curved spine, hugging her knees. The sight of his wife soaking wet and broken because he'd told her not to come home ripped at him.

His pulse thrummed thickly in his neck as his chest squeezed. Not a muscle in her twitched as he stepped within three feet of her crumbled frame.

"Sadie," his strained voice came out barely a whisper.

He didn't think it was possible for her to slump farther, but she did, the back of her neck bowing so deeply it looked painful.

That movement did him in. He collapsed next to her and was a second from collecting her balled body in his arms, but her devastated eyes kept him at bay. "How'd you find me?"

"Buddy mentioned you bought more than the three flower plants you showed me."

She winced at his words, her vacant gaze drifting over the water. "So you know."

"Yeah," he rasped.

"But it doesn't matter, does it? This is irreparable. I was so consumed with grief over losing them"—her moisture glazed eyes blinked to his—"that I've already lost you too."

Even though it felt like his insides were being shredded, his answer sat stagnant in his open mouth because he honestly wasn't sure. They'd shifted so far away from each other that he wasn't certain they'd find firm footing again. In his silence, Sadie hunched over her knees.

"That's what I thought."

His elbows hit his thighs as a halting exhale blew over the placid water in front of him. Neither of them spoke for a long time, and soon the steely skies began to release their moisture. Thick drops darkened the azure of his T-shirt—the one Sadie had bought him because she said it highlighted the blue of his eyes.

When the warm liquid on his cheeks contrasted with those which dotted his exposed forearms and legs, it took several seconds to realize they were his own tears. The summer rainstorm picked up in strength, plopping and bouncing drops that mangled the lake's even surface. His eyes pressed together before he ran a hand over his face.

"We have to try, right?" His voice was as hoarse as the frogs who'd joyously come out to play in the sheeting rain.

He could feel Sadie's gaze on his face but couldn't look away from the blurring landscape in front of him.

"If that's what you want."

His muscles turned automatically, taking in his wife's dew dropped eyelashes. "That's not what you want?"

She bit the corner of her lip. "Too much of our relationship has been what I want. You're right. I haven't considered you enough. From now on, I need you to tell me what you want— what you need—so things can be more even between us."

"I've always wanted you, Sadie. I don't think I know how to not want you." He paused. "But you've been the one who's put me at an arm's length. Are you sure you still want me? Want us?"

Her whispered words were almost absorbed by the storm. "I miss us."

Clark's chest lightened a fraction. "Me too."

The rhythmic sound of rainfall and the harsh rasp of his own strained breathing were the only sounds that entered Clark's ears for a long time.

"So what do we do now?" Sadie pushed a matted strand of hair away from her face.

Clark hesitated only for a second, but then he let the words he wanted to say fall from his lips. "We've got that appointment tomorrow at nine."

"Yes," she said, her eyes determined and focused in a way that told him she intended to put as much effort into repairing their relationship as she used in the OR.

His words scratched from his throat as the rain began to ease up. "I really need you to talk to me. I know it's hard on you, but I need that from you."

Pain settled in the hollows of her cheeks, but her gaze remained insistent. "I understand. I'm sorry I didn't try harder before, but I will now."

"And I need you not to run here"—he gestured to the lake—"when you're upset and leave me blindsided and confused."

She swallowed with a nod. "I'll try."

This burning tension seized his lungs, and he had to settle his gaze over the water and focus on the simple act of breathing for a few minutes. The gentle sensation of softening rain nurtured his aching back muscles.

With a sigh, he wiped the remaining rainfall off his face. "All right."

Sadie's gaze was already focused on him when he turned to her, though she remained silent.

When he understood that she was waiting on him to tell her what their next step should be, that she was allowing him to take the lead in this, her consideration sent warmth surging through his veins. "I think the best thing now would be to go home."

"Are you sure?" The uncertainty in her eyes made his heart squeeze.

Instinctually, his hand raised to frame his wife's lovely face. "Yes, love. Let's go home."

·CHAPTER 31·

Sadie picked at the seam of her scrubs as Clark finished telling Dr. Shah—or Tara, as she insisted they call her—a rough overview of the last year of their lives. It had been easiest to allow him to answer all the general questions, knowing that soon Tara would ask her direct ones. Though the office's neutral cream and grey tones had likely been chosen for their soothing effect, even the artistically painted jade lilypad she'd been staring at didn't quell the anxiety bounding through Sadie's veins.

"Okay," their new therapist said. "We obviously can't tackle a year's worth of topics in a single session. My understanding is that you two are on the same page regarding wanting to try to work this out. Is that correct?"

The emphatic way Clark said "yes" lit Sadie from the inside out.

"Yes," she said, eyes darting and snagging on his.

"Great." Tara folded her hands in her lap. "Then what I'd like to do is ask you both to imagine your preferred outcome of these sessions. Keep in mind that whatever you say today can morph and change over time. Your answer isn't going to be written in stone. It's just a jumping off point. Sadie, what would you like to come of our time together?"

She'd been anticipating something more challenging, but this was the easiest thing Tara could have asked her. "I want to be with Clark."

Tara slightly tilted her chin. "Could you qualify that for me? What does that look like to you?"

Sadie sat up with an inhale. "I want our relationship to be as strong as it was after Lottie was born." Her gaze gravitated toward her husband's again. "But I also want things to be different. I want to be more considerate of Clark's needs. I want to make sure that he knows how much I love him. How much he matters to me. I want him to be happy. Before all this happened, I was so happy, but I'm not sure he was."

"Clark, do you want to respond to that?"

His brilliant blue eyes never wavered from hers. "I was happy, love. Up until you started closing yourself off, our life had been perfect. At times, I was unsure it was real."

The corner of her mouth pulled up. "Sometimes, I thought we lived in an alternate dimension."

"Really?" The question was more of a surprised breath.

She slid her hand off her scrub pants onto the microfiber loveseat between them—an invitation but not a command. "Yeah."

Clark didn't hesitate to interlace his long fingers with hers, and Sadie reveled in the familiar scrape of his hardened palm.

Tara let the moment expand before directing their conversation again. "And Clark, what would you like from our time together?"

Her husband's hand stiffened as he looked away. "I . . ." He swallowed hard and his collarbones tightened.

"Clark?" She worried that his idea of the future didn't match hers.

His eyes slowly rose to hers. "I don't want to have any more children."

She blinked as her eyebrows twitched, drawing her hand back. "But having two kids was always your vision for our family."

"We can't be a family if we aren't together, and trying to give Lottie a sibling is costing us our relationship. I'm not willing to make that sacrifice anymore. It's causing too much harm." His face slackened. "It's hurting us both too much."

"But—"

"Sadie, can you acknowledge that even though you and Clark had one plan for your future, he might want to change that plan?" Tara asked.

Her gaze volleyed between their therapist's neutral face and her husband's painfully scrunched brow.

"Do I have to like it?" she asked Tara.

"No. Of course not," she said. "You just have to acknowledge that this is what he wants at this point in time." Tara let a pause settle between them before gently asking, "Do you want to explain to Clark why this change bothers you?"

The single sip of coffee she'd managed to stomach this morning was trying to come back up and choke her. "I'll try."

She took a measured breath, reminding herself that the only way to keep Clark in her life was to open up her body and let him see all her ugly insides—to be brutally honest.

"I never wanted children," Sadie told their therapist. "Actually, that's not true. I never thought I could have children because it didn't seem to be an option for me. I'd chosen to pursue this incredibly challenging career that I loved, and I knew I wouldn't want to stop working to have a family. But then I met Clark, and all the obstacles I'd set up for myself, that society had set up for me, seemed to fall away. He always made everything so easy, so effortless. He made this dream I couldn't have even imagined a reality, and that's why I tried so hard this last year to fulfill the last part of it for him. For us."

She cautioned a glance at her husband, and an unmistakable dampness sheened over his expressive eyes.

"I love you, Clark." Her voice cracked as tears collected in her own eyes. "I've always loved you. I just"—she shook her head and an errant drop raced down her nose before she could swipe at it—"I got lost in all of this. I'm sorry."

Her face was pressed against the coolness of her husband's collar before she registered that her fists had balled the fabric over his heart. Clark's arms wove around her, gripping her securely. Her husband's strong heartbeat pulsing against her temple helped quiet the tumultuous emotions reverberating through her body.

"But that's exactly why we have to stop, love." His voice was hoarse. "I can't have this anymore. I can't have you suffering and me helpless in the distance and then trying to deal with my sadness on my own." He leaned back to gently chase the tears from her cheeks with his thumb. "I'd like to spend our time working on getting us to a better place. You need to fix bones. I need to fix us."

"I want to fix us, too, but . . ." The rest of the words—wondering if he'd be happy with just her, wondering if she was enough on her own—slammed against the bones inside her skull, but as much as she tried, they wouldn't pass over her lips.

A solemn smile crossed Clark's face. "You and Lottie are enough for me. As long as I have you two, everything else is just a bonus."

◊◊◊

The fact that Sadie was able to focus on her midmorning operation after the emotional therapy session with Clark was a testament to her professionalism. By the time she broke for lunch, nearly all of the clouded sensation that hovered throughout her clavicular stabilization surgery had dissipated.

Baylee handed Sadie her phone and pager. "Two personal texts, one from Dr. Bauer—which was non-urgent, and three pages I passed on to your resident on the floor."

"Thank you." She pulled on her white coat and took the two devices from her circulating nurse. "See you in thirty minutes."

"We'll be ready for you, Dr. Carmichael."

Clipping her pager to the waistband of her scrubs, she looked over the long text from Linus, barely keeping a barking laugh from leaving her mouth. Apparently, Josh had attempted to air his complaints about Sadie being late to surgery to one of the older members of their practice this morning during rounds. In front of the entire ortho floor, Dr. Olivares had roasted Josh about a time he'd missed the first half of a surgery—which Sadie hadn't known about—because Josh had been caught in a storage closet with one of the nurses from the ER.

Linus had typed, "And I quote, Ricardo said, 'If you can be late for having your *chorra* two inches into, let's hope, a consenting staff member, Dr. Carmichael can sleep in one day.'" Then Linus detailed that Dr. Olivares had shaken his head and muttered something in Spanish that caused one of the nearby nurses to burst into laughter. Linus admitted he didn't know what Ricardo had said, but it probably wasn't complimentary.

Sadie: *That's hilarious. I wish I could have been there.*

She snorted after sending Linus the text, imagining the scene as she climbed the stairs to the hospital doctor's lounge. She quickly toggled to the message from Parker.

Parker: *Hey toots. This is me being a caring, non-emotionally stunted friend and checking on you.*

Sadie had sent a quick message on the way home from Lake Trail Park yesterday afternoon stating she didn't need to crash on Parker's couch again. Since her friend had been at the hospital on shift, she'd lit up Sadie's phone with a wide variety of celebratory GIFs.

Sadie: *Lol. I'm good. Thanks for checking.*

Out of habit, she saved the message from Clark for last. Pausing twenty feet from the lounge door and pressing herself against the hallway wall, she took a deep breath before reading it.

Clark: *I love you, Sadie. Thank you for this morning.*

On impulse, she hit call, and when Clark picked up, he sounded winded. "Hey, love." The tone, inflection, and ease with which her pet name tumbled off his tongue made her heart thump in her neck.

"Hi." Her voice almost cracked.

"Lottie was just asking about you. Right before she decided to go full-sprint toward the poison ivy in the back trees and I had to catch her. Say hi to Mama, little love."

"Hi, Mama" sounded over the phone, and Sadie had to look up and blink back the wetness flooding over her eyes.

How long had it been since she'd called just to check up on her family during the day? Too long.

"Are you having a good afternoon?" she asked.

"We are." Sadie could almost see Clark's smile from the sound of his voice. "We had quesadillas for lunch"—in the background Lottie cheered—"and pretty soon this one's going to take a nap, and I'll work, and then we're meeting Omar and Victor at the park to play before you get home."

There was no doubt in Sadie's bones that the minute she finished with her afternoon surgery, she'd arrow her car straight home. "That sounds really nice."

The oddest feeling flushed through her bloodstream at having such a routine midday call with her husband. If anyone overheard their conversation, they'd think nothing revolutionary was taking place, but in Sadie's heart she felt each little piece of their broken relationship lining up. Soon, she'd be able to apply reduction clamps, eventually a plate and some screws, and then allow it to heal under its own power.

It wouldn't always be this easy, she knew that, too, but today, it was working. She was trying, and so was Clark.

"I can't wait to see you." Clark's earnest words sent warmth sprinting down her spine.

"Me too," she said. "I miss you." Logic had no standing, even as it shouted at her that she'd seen her husband a mere three hours ago; it had already felt like thirty-six.

At her waist, her pager sounded.

"Is that you?" Clark asked.

"Yeah." A reluctant sigh left her lips. "And I need to try to eat something before I'm due back in the OR."

"Go take care of yourself. We'll be here when you get home." He paused. "We're not going anywhere." She caught the deeper meaning woven into her husband's words.

"Okay." She wanted to say more, but her tight throat wouldn't let the syllables out.

"I love you, Sadie." Clark's voice reflected the affection bouncing around in every cell in her body.

Everything in her felt lighter, felt aligned, as she responded with the simple words she'd been using for years. Emotion laced them as their meaning resonated in her muscles. After a long period of grief-driven separation, she knew her heart was finally speaking directly to Clark's.

"I love you too."

·CHAPTER 32·

Three months later

The same icy air conditioning that she'd vacated moments ago upon leaving her office on the other side of Durham Medical Center's campus blasted Sadie's face once she entered the building that held Tara's office. Even though the first day of fall had been two days ago, mother nature had decided not to relinquish her stranglehold on summer.

Inside the lobby, Clark stood waiting for her. That usual breathlessness that accompanied seeing her husband swept her body. With his hands tucked into dark jeans and a black polo stretching over every muscle, he looked particularly delicious today. She caught a mirrored expression on his face as his gaze dragged slowly over her cerulean blouse and pearl white slacks. Since she'd met Reagan for their bi-weekly mentorship coffee early this morning, she'd left the house while Clark had still been sleeping.

Apprehension and excitement fought for first place in her body. Last week, she'd encountered a smiling Clark before therapy only for them to end up disagreeing in their session. Later that evening, a shouting match had broken out that had woken Lottie. Part of her had to acknowledge that even screaming at each other was slightly better than the stoic silence and avoidance that had been their status quo several months ago, but she definitely preferred days like this one. The last few days, she and Clark had seemed to operate like two sides of the same mind.

He leaned in to give her a simple kiss before palming the back of her head, securing her close to him, his lips lingering over her ear. "Tell me you don't have another appointment right after this."

His hoarse, commanding voice sent anticipation shuddering through all her muscles.

"Not until two."

"Good," he said and then gave the crook of her neck a split-second suck before releasing her. "I want to make good use of Lottie's remaining preschool hours before pickup."

Sadie could feel her blush racing from her chest to the tips of her ears. A smug, satisfied look crossed Clark's face before he grabbed her hand and tugged her to the elevator bank. As the wood paneled metal box began its ascent, she couldn't help but fidget her free arm.

"Thank you."

When she looked over, her husband's eyes were on her.

"For what?"

"I know meeting with Tara isn't your favorite thing." He squeezed their interlocked fingers.

It wasn't, but she couldn't deny that working—truly working—on their relationship had strengthened the connection she had with her husband. Sadie didn't think it was possible, but she felt more in line with Clark that she'd even been before. They still shared that undeniable physical attraction and mutual respect, but now they also shared the dark and sticky corners of their hearts. Most of the time, it was downright terrifying, but afterwards they were stitched together more tightly than before, making each hard step inarguably worth it.

Other relationships had also improved once she'd learned to open her mouth and let out what she was thinking and feeling. She and Parker had started spending about half of their time on their nights out actually discussing their lives instead of just talking about the best cases from the week. And with Tara and Clark's support, Sadie was able to set some much-needed boundaries with her mother. They still spoke, but Penelope understood that if she was in the mood to cut Sadie down, their call could come to a brisk end.

A dinging resonated in the small space a second before the elevator doors opened. "No," she conceded. "But you are, so it's worth it."

Clark smirked as they walked down the carpeted hallway. "Don't lie to me, love. We all know surgery is your favorite thing."

"You're tied for first," she said, before amending that statement. "Actually, if you want honesty, it's a three-way tie with Lottie."

Her husband brought her knuckles to his smiling lips for a quick kiss while she pushed through the glass door to their therapist's office.

◊◊◊

Two hours later, they were wrapped up in each other's arms on top of their bed. Clark dreamily ran his hand down her spine as he watched the birds swoop from tree to tree through the windows to the backyard.

"Do you think they'll notice if I come back for the rest of my appointments wearing different pants?"

Her husband's breathless laugh bounced her head. "I had no idea zippers could be so delicate."

A smile stretched her lips as she looked up. "You were acting like we hadn't seen each other naked in weeks instead of less than twenty-four hours."

He let out a playful, dismissive noise before he rolled on top of her, his arms bracketing her head. "That didn't count. I was half asleep when you woke me up after your call shift last night." His kisses rained over her ear, trailing down her throat. A halting breath dragged into her chest as one of his hands slithered down her side. "Besides, I can't see that flush of yours when it's dark."

In a fraction of a second, everything went from feeling so blissfully perfect to seven directions of wrong. The achiness she'd been fighting since yesterday doubled down in her back muscles as fatigue swept through her. She'd ordered an extra shot in her Red Eye at the cafe this morning to counteract the bone-sucking lethargy that had seemed to haunt her for the last few days, but now it was back, full force.

Clark immediately registered the swift change. "What's wrong?"

"I'm sorry. I'm just exhausted."

The corner of Clark's mouth lifted as sympathy and adoration flooded his eyes. "You didn't get much sleep last night, and we missed lunch. Why don't you get dressed for the rest of your afternoon appointments? I'll make us something to eat."

"Would you pour me a bowl of Cinnamon Toast Crunch?"

Clark's laugh washed over her body. "Sure, love." He kissed her shoulder and then climbed off the bed.

While her husband made himself a sandwich in the kitchen, Sadie retied her very disheveled ponytail and found a pair of grey slacks to replace her damaged ones. Sudden nausea rolled through her like a wave tumbling to the shore, and her head snapped up. A very pale, wide-eyed version of herself looked back at her in the bathroom mirror.

I can't be.

Opening the cabinet beneath her sink, she found the two purple boxes in the same place they'd been for months.

Somehow, she made it down the stairs even though it felt like all her bones had been replaced with a slightly gelatinous substance. Her hands were trembling, specifically the one that clenched the hard plastic.

Midday sun streamed through the kitchen windows and bounced off Clark's bare shoulders as he whistled, piling various deli meats onto wheat bread. This odd déjà vu overwhelmed her—Clark whistling, in the kitchen, jeans slung low on his trim hips.

"I'm pregnant."

Mustard squirted all over his bread and made a haphazard line on the counter before her husband's fist released the yellow bottle. "What?"

"I'm pregnant." She lifted her shaking palm, showing him the deep-indigo cross.

Clark stood frozen. "But I wore a condom every time."

"Yeah, I know . . . but—" She took a deep inhale as her heart tried to reach the upper limits of tachycardia. "No form of birth control is ever one-hundred percent effective."

Weighted knowledge hovered between them, remembering how Lottie had been conceived.

Clark broke the tension with this jubilant half-laugh/half-shout. He rushed to her, his hands framing her waist before he hesitated. "Will it hurt you if I pick you up?"

Even though she still felt achy and a little nauseous, she shook her head no. She didn't have the heart to deny Clark when he was this incandescent. Sadie took a short spin around the kitchen before he delicately placed her on her toes, keeping his arms snug around her.

"Sadie, this is our baby." His words were whispered over her lips.

She could feel her eyebrows twin together as more than a year's worth of doubt, pain, and grief flashed forward with that four-letter word.

Her husband shook his head before tenderly kissing the space between her brows. "No. Not this time. Not this one. This one we get to keep."

"You don't know that." Her voice pitched. "I could miscarry again, and then I'll have to drive around town and add a fourth plant everywhere."

"No, love." His lips brushed hers so softly. "Then *we'd* drive around together. You're not alone anymore, and neither am I. Anything that comes our way, we face it together."

When he rested his forehead on hers, Sadie closed her eyes and breathed in Clark's familiar wood-tinged scent. That impulse to wrap herself around him surged through her muscles, and she gripped his back, pulling them close to the point that no air could separate their bodies. Her husband's breath broke over her neck as he held her just as tightly.

"It's going to be okay," he whispered.

She felt her head dip in affirmation.

It *was* going to be okay.

Even if the worst happened. Even if she lost this life, too, her relationship with her husband would survive. It would be devastating to go through a fourth time, but Sadie knew that on the other side of that heartbreak, Clark would be there.

She released her vise-grip and leaned back a little. "Okay."

"All right." His grin was soft, supportive, comforting.

Nervously, her hand flitted to the medallion resting just above her neckline. Even after they'd decided to change their family plan, she'd never taken off the necklace. Clark watched her fingertips rub the golden metal circle.

"Tell me, love." His hand gently framed her face. "Are we having a boy or a girl?"

Out of the swirling maelstrom of emotions over finding out she was pregnant, a single one shined the brightest. It took over the rest like an ever-expanding cloud, tumbling and covering the sky.

"A girl."

Clark's full dimpled smile mirrored the elation on her face. "Perfect."

·EPILOGUE·

Two years later

"You be good for Daddy today," Lottie instructed, her overfilled backpack teetering dangerously to one side as she stooped to hug her sister.

Avery's pudgy little fingers gripped Lottie's legs in an enthusiastic grip, and Lottie smiled, rubbing her sister's short dark hair. "I love you too, bug."

Ever since they'd shared the news with Lottie that she would become a big sister, she'd taken her role very seriously. After Avery's birth fifteen months ago, Lottie had helped with most diaper changes and bottle feeds. She'd pushed the stroller, held her sister's hand as she'd learned to walk, and when it came time to teach Avery the challenging world of cutlery, Lottie had explained that blackberry jam was the best pancake topping, even though Avery preferred blueberry.

He and Sadie had waited until Avery's twenty-week sonogram to explain the changes in their family to then-three-year-old Lottie. Clark could still feel how firmly Sadie's fingers gripped his as each grey organ was measured and checked on the screen before Avery was determined to be "perfectly healthy." Two days later, Sadie hadn't come home after work, and he'd panicked. Once Parker had arrived to watch Lottie, he'd found his wife in the snow at Peaceably Park, weeping in front of the trio of gerber daisy plants with her hands pressed to her belly. He'd simply sat on the hard, icy ground and wrapped his arms around her until she stopped shaking.

As much as they had both been nervous through Avery's pregnancy, Tara had helped them to focus on the joyful moments. Like when Sadie really started showing and Lottie would kiss her belly every day before Sadie left for work. Or when they got to see Avery over and over again because Sadie had more frequent appointments with her OB, including extra ultrasounds. Every time Clark heard that reassuring whooshing of a heartbeat, his spine settled.

Even with all the extra stress, their relationship continued to strengthen. It wobbled at times, when they argued or tried to fall back into destructive habits, but before any real damage had been done, one of them would pull the other out. They'd falter, learn from their mistakes, and then spend heartfelt intimate minutes making it up to each other.

Avery's giggle pulled him back to the sidewalk. Lottie was picking her sister up in a rib-squeezing hug.

Holding Sadie's hand while watching his children embrace, Clark didn't think he could experience greater happiness. The only thing clouding it was the approaching sound of the vehicle that would take Lottie away for a few hours. Even though the deep diesel rumble of the school bus was still far away at the entrance to their large neighborhood, Clark felt his chest squeeze tighter than a wood vise. Beside him, he knew Sadie was having a similar internal struggle as her wrist twisted more times than it had before her uncomplicated delivery.

"Maybe I should have taken the whole day off," Sadie whispered.

"No." He brushed a kiss over his wife's temple. "It's better you're in surgery. It'll help distract you, and then by the time you get home, they'll be done with nap, homework, quiet time, and we can all play."

Sadie nodded absently, her eyes trained on their street and watching for the bus. Lottie was showing Avery the information card that she wore on a yarn necklace, telling her all the details about kindergarten she'd learned from the meet-and-greet night five days ago—her teacher's name, that her cubby had a purple starfish on it, and that the cafeteria had streamers in the school colors hanging from the ceiling. Avery babbled a smiling response to her sister's every word, and Clark's heart squeezed, thinking of the many conversations his girls would share for years to come.

"How are you so calm right now?" his wife asked in a hushed voice.

He pulled his attention from his daughters to meet Sadie's anxious gaze. "I'm not. Inside I'm a mess, but she's so excited for kindergarten that I don't want her to feel nervous because I'm nervous."

His wife gave her single curt nod, and he watched her cover her vulnerability with her trademark strength a second before the big yellow bus turned the corner to their street. Sadie pulled her shoulders back, even as a short breath punched from her chest.

"You're going to have the best day." His wife pulled Lottie into a tight embrace that continued until the exhaustive heave of the bus pulling to a stop sounded beside them. "I can't wait to hear about it when I get home. I love you."

"Love you too." Lottie grinned.

Avery started toddling toward the open bus doors, and Sadie let go of Lottie to pick her up before she stepped off the curb.

"Have a great first day, little love. I'll see you after school." He crouched to pull Lottie into an embrace that rivaled his wife's.

"Love you, Daddy."

Clark kissed her ponytail before he forced his arms to let go. "I love you too. Hop up on the first step, and we'll get a picture."

Lottie practically flew to the bus stairs, smiled more brightly than her face had ever stretched, and posed for her "first day of school photo." He felt like a part of himself was being sawed away as her glittery tennis shoes climbed higher until she disappeared between the high-backed seats.

"Drop off will be at 3:15 p.m.," the bus driver stated with a grin before closing the doors.

Sadie had found Lottie at the window six rows back and was waving vigorously, prompting Avery to copy her. Their eldest daughter beamed from her seat and returned the wave until the bus pulled out of sight.

Beside him, Sadie's long exhale was halting and ragged.

"It's like part of your heart is walking around outside your body," he offered. He'd learned through their time with Tara that offering his verbal explanation of his feelings often helped Sadie with her own.

Her pale green eyes caught his before her hard swallow. "That's exactly it. And something about her getting on the bus has a finality to it. I know she's only five and still little, but she's not a baby anymore."

"No, she's not." He ran his hand down her arm and interwove their fingers.

His thumb gently pressed against the thin rose gold chain of the bracelet his wife never took off. Before Avery had been born, he'd had it custom made by a local jeweler. Nestled in the center of the three rose gold circles were round diamonds—yellow, white, and yellow.

Sadie squeezed his hand while the etched lines on her face softened.

"Luckily, this one still is," she said.

A small smile tugged at his mouth as Sadie burrowed her face in Avery's neck and tightened her grip on their youngest.

Hand in hand, they walked up their driveway while Avery babbled on Sadie's hip. His wife tried to flip her forearm before remembering her fingers were intertwined with his.

"She'll be okay." He pressed a kiss to the inside of her wrist and then tried another tactic. "Remember when the kids go to bed tonight, you're meeting with Parker to plan her bachelorette party."

It still brought a strange chuckle to his lips that his wife's best friend had ended up dating and was now engaged to the man he'd accused Sadie of having an affair with.

"Oh, yeah. Will you be okay by yourself tonight?"

That expansive feeling kept trying to test the limits of his ribs. "Yeah. I was going to work on a new design."

Sadie's eyes lit over her scrubs. "I can't wait to see it."

His side-hobby-turned-business had been so steady over the last few years that he wondered if, when Avery joined her sister on that big yellow bus, he'd return to work as a carpenter. Right now, that was still the plan, but he'd learned that plans sometimes need to be altered. Sometimes, joy bounded into your life with stark unexpectedness and other times, grief ripped the flesh off your bones.

The best thing to do was enjoy what small moments you had.

Even if that was as simple as holding your wife's hand on a balmy September morning.

It was these little moments stacked upon each other that made up the good in your life. A quick kiss goodbye. The first laugh of your baby daughter. Waking up to your wife snuggling against you.

Sadie sighed loudly as they reached the garage, staring at her packed and ready crossover. Though his wife had just been voted into her third year as the director of orthopedic surgery—unanimously this time—Clark could see she was reluctant to leave them today.

The corner of his mouth tipped up. "You're going to have a good day too. And we'll all be here when you get home." He paused, letting emotion fill his words. "We're always right here."

Silently, she bobbed her head before letting go of his hand in favor of pulling his shoulder toward her, careful not to crush Avery between them. When his wife's soft kisses lingered over his lips, he understood that Sadie was telling him, in her own perfect way, how much she loved him.

ACKNOWLEDGMENTS

Most importantly, I want to thank those who were brave enough to share their stories so I could tell Sadie and Clark's. Though I will never fully understand the heartbreak you've experienced, I truly hope that this book, and those like it, will help open conversations that otherwise might not have been spoken.

As always, I'm grateful to my incredible developmental editor and proofreader, Rachel Garber. Thank you for your kindness, flexibility, and always championing my work. I'm also thankful for my line editor, Emily Poole, and copy editor, Rebecca Jaycox. A big thank you to Lisa Wittrock for beta reading this novel. Karri Klawiter's amazing design graces this cover yet again. I'm extremely appreciative of the awesome people in the book community who support and promote my work. And thank you to readers Morna and Chelsea for contributing tattoo design ideas.

I could not do this without the huge support of my family. AJ, Brooke, and Alex, you make every day infinitely better. Thank you also to my parents, my extended family, and Jackie, April, and Chelsea for their endless support.

My gratitude is immense for you, dear reader, for picking up this book. I truly hope that though this novel centered on such a painful subject, you still enjoyed the story. Thank you so much for spending time out of your life with my characters, and with me.

ABOUT THE AUTHOR

Laura Langa strives to write stories that pull at her readers' heartstrings and create relatable characters you can't help but root for. As a former medical professional, she uses her experience in the field to inform her writing. Laura loves trees and all things green, hates flossing but forces herself to do it every night, drinks tea—not coffee, and believes that salt air can often cure a bad mood.

Visit her website at www.LauraLanga.com
Subscribe to her newsletter for the latest details at www.LauraLanga.com/Newsletter
Follow on Instagram and Facebook @LauraLangaWrites